I0676536

R.I.P.

(Vlad V Series)

The Death of a Vampire

By Mit Sandru

Chivileri Publishing

Copyright © 2013 by Dumitru Sandru

This is a fictional story. All names, persons,

organizations, businesses, places, and occurrences

are fictitious and are the imagination of the author.

Any resemblances to actual people or events are

completely coincidental.

Acknowledgements

Many thanks to Dr. Adrian and my family

Table of Contents

The previous book in this series is *Vampire (Vlad V Series)*

Meeting a vampire isn't something that happens every night, even on the New York City subway. But never in her wildest dreams did Cat ever expect to meet a vampire or survive an encounter with one. Instead, she became his confidant. Why was she so lucky?

6

Chapter 1. A Person of Interest

In an unmarked office at the US Department of Homeland Security branch in New York City, Special Agent John Miller (not his real name) thumbed through the files retrieved from FBI archives. He knew this file very well, because he was the last agent in the FBI to handle the Vlad Draculesti case. As a matter of fact, he started his career with this case in 1971, when the FBI Director J. Edgar Hoover personally picked him for that assignment; he was to take over from the previous agent, Frank Hulbert, who had died of a heart attack.

As it happened, Director Hoover had met Mr. Draculesti in 1955 and remembered him from an encounter in 1933. Twenty-two years later, the man hadn't changed a bit: He was the same youthful, twenty-something rich man. Director Hoover thought that Vlad Draculesti might be a Communist bloc spy, sent to the US in the 1930s.

Soon after the file was opened in 1955, the first assigned agent, Rod Tiller – who also died of a heart attack – discovered even more troubling evidence about Mr. Draculesti. Agent Tiller found a photograph of him from Ellis Island, dated 1908, and the photo showed the same youthful, twenty-something arriving in America as an emigrant from

Romania. Who was this man, Vlad Draculesti, who did not seem to age?

In his time on the case, Miller had done a diligent job of investigating Vlad Draculesti. Unfortunately, Mr. Draculesti was not a spy – only fabulously rich. The main suspicion surrounding his eternal youth began to crumble when he began aging, and, by the late 1970s, the FBI closed the case.

Miller knew better. He pursued the case on his own and found a witness identifying Vlad Draculesti as a vampire. In spite of that, Miller did not have enough convincing evidence to ask for the case to be reopened. He was a patient man and waited for the right opportunity to investigate Vlad Draculesti again. Since the FBI would not investigate him, the Department of Homeland Security or the NSA might, if the right evidence were presented.

At the first opportunity, he transferred from the FBI to the US Department of Homeland Security. Once there, and with new advanced face recognition software on Homeland's supercomputers, he opened a new search on Vlad Draculesti using the photos he had of him. The computer returned the verdict. With a confidence level of 99.9%, the Vlad Draculesti of 1908 was the same man as the one from 1955, and 1971. The last official picture in the FBI file, from 1977, was the same man as well, but the aging process had begun.

That was enough proof to request a new investigation, and then the big surprise came.

The supercomputer found the same man in a picture dating from 1851. For some reason, every photograph found in libraries and archives, even from those early years of photography, was in the supercomputer's database. That picture from 1851 was of a group of men posing in front of the Crystal Palace during the London World Exhibition. One of the individuals was Vlad Draculesti. The confidence level the computer assigned to this new piece of evidence was 99.8%. This was the icing on the cake.

Miller knew Randy Jaworski, assistant deputy director of the US intelligence community, from his early years in the FBI. They had started as federal agents at the same time, except that Randy became the assistant deputy director at Homeland, while Miller remained an agent. He approached Randy, bypassing several layers of management, and presented him the file with the new information on Vlad Draculesti, provided by the Homeland supercomputer.

Although Assistant Deputy Director Jaworski laughed at first when he recalled the case, he stopped laughing when he saw the information. Even an assistant deputy director cannot argue with a supercomputer. He opened a case on Vlad Draculesti and put John Miller in charge of it. Miller was back on Draculesti's investigation, and not a moment too soon.

To familiarize himself anew with this unusual case, Special Agent Miller read the file and inspected a new photo of Mr. Draculesti taken just two days before. Vlad Draculesti looked dapper – tall and slim, dressed in black, pale, and with his white hair combed back like a mafia don. An old don. Miller smirked. He hated this filthy-rich man. But he had plans for Vlad Draculesti – life-shattering plans for this vampire.

Another incredible and startling piece of information about this man – or vampire – was a grainy surveillance video that had become available just days before the case was reopened. He viewed the video a dozen times and pondered it. Draculesti was a person of special interest for Homeland Security and the NSA now, thanks to Miller's tenacity. But it seemed that someone at the top knew the true identity of blue-blooded Vlad Draculesti. Miller never reported this, and there was no such information in the file, but the expediency with which this case was opened made him wonder if the man-in-charge-at-the-top chose him for this case, rather than the other way around. He didn't care. What was important was that he was back officially investigating Draculesti again.

Was this karma or pure coincidence? He had started on this case at the beginning of his career, and now he was about to retire on the same case. He had had high hopes for himself back then, but he got old, and nothing panned out the way he had wished over the years. All his talents and brilliance were smothered by incompetent superiors who had blocked the promotions that he deserved, along with the better money he needed to provide for a comfortable retirement. After three divorces, he had no money put aside, and his pension was not enough for him and his ex-wives, who took a bite out of it. Then a thought crossed his mind: What if the filthy-rich Vlad Draculesti was behind his lackluster career? Yes, that made sense, and now he was in a position to extract his pound of flesh, and then some.

The other two agents assigned to his team were to use aliases, just as he was. That was unusual, since this was not a CIA mission. The secrecy was over the top as well. The windowless office had three steel desks, each with computers bolted onto them. The keypads with built-in mouse devices had thumb-identification access capabilities. This was to prevent espionage. Even the access to this office had a thumb reader, an ID card swipe, and a digital pad for the access codes. Triple security entry was used only on *super-secret* cases. Mr. Draculesti's case did not warrant this kind of security and secrecy, unless it was the video that spooked the big boys. Perhaps it was the potential military aspect of Draculesti being an alien? No, he was just a blood-sucking vampire.

It was nine o'clock in the morning, and it was time for his other two agents to arrive. Just as he thought of that, he could see from the security window on his computer that the door was being accessed. The outside camera fed the image of the man accessing the door onto his computer screen. Miller did not recognize him. Behind him was another man he did not recognize, waiting his turn to access the security pad and enter the office. Tailgating was prohibited.

Miller stood up and waited.

The first man entered, showed his ID, and introduced himself: "Agent Johnson, reporting for duty."

"Special Agent Miller. Glad to meet you, Agent Johnson." Miller shook Johnson's hand. Just like Miller's name, Johnson was an alias. He looked more like a Gonzalez, big and beefy, in his mid-forties.

The second man came in and showed his ID. "Agent Smith, reporting for duty, sir."

"Special Agent Miller. Glad to meet you, Agent Smith." Miller shook Smith's hand. Smith looked like a paramilitary, solidly built, in his thirties, with a short blond haircut. "This is Agent Johnson." The two men shook hands, and they all sat down.

"Gentlemen," Miller began, "as you know, this is a top-secret assignment. Our names are aliases, and we don't know each other or have ever met before. Each one of us is given a computer, a smartphone, ID and passwords for accessing them. The information about this case is in this file." He waved the folder. "And the information has been digitized and available on your computers. Please read it, and then let's discuss it."

The other two agents took off their jackets, loosened their ties, and set to diligently read the files on their computers.

"Is this for real?" asked Johnson, after they finished reading.

"J. Edgar Hoover thought something was suspicious enough to open a dossier on Vlad Draculesti," said Smith.

"He had this case opened in 1955, and then it gathered dust from 1977 until now," said Miller, omitting that he had been the agent on the case from 1971 to 1977 and that he had spied on Draculesti on his own after the investigation was closed.

"It could have been a look-alike with the same name," said Johnson, furrowing his brow. "Maybe father and son?"

"Father and son looking youthful from 1908 until 1972?" questioned Miller.

"Dick Clark looked the same for over fifty years," replied Johnson.

"This Draculesti was from an era when plastic surgery was not as advanced as it is today," said Miller.

"Yes, but the guy is old now. Is this picture recent?" asked Johnson, pointing to his screen.

"From a few days ago," confirmed Miller.

"The resemblance is close. But it couldn't be the same guy." Johnson shook his head.

"Computer analysis verifies that the man in 1851 is the same man in 1908, in 1955, and in 1972," said Miller. "Furthermore, the computer simulation shows that the latest picture of Mr. Draculesti is the same man, although aged."

"But, according to his bio, he was born in 1910." Johnson scrolled through his computer to make sure the DOB was right. "I don't understand what the mystery is about him."

"With a falsified birth certificate, he could have started a new life as the son of a Vlad Draculesti from Ellis Island in 1908," said Miller. "Homeland Security places a lot of confidence in its computers, and soon it may have picture of everyone in the US in its database, along with their fingerprints and DNA. What if Vlad Draculesti is the same person all along?"

Agent Johnson scoffed. "The original FBI case was to discover if Mr. Draculesti was a communist spy, which turned out to be false."

"Yes, but his life span was also a factor back then. It didn't pan out because he aged," said Agent Miller. "What if he hasn't aged and he is disguising himself as an older man?"

Agent Johnson's eyes opened wide but then narrowed suspiciously.

"Yes. This time, our case is to find out who this guy is and if he is the same man from way back then," said Agent Miller. "He speaks with an accent, a European accent, which is not surprising since he emigrated from Romania in 1908. If he were born here, he wouldn't have an accent."

"So who is this guy, really, sir?" asked Smith.

"Please, Smith, don't call me sir."

"Understood, Special Agent Miller."

"And from now on, don't use 'agent,' either. Let's address each other by our last names."

"Yes, s–. Yes, Miller."

"Better." Miller continued, "If he is an emigrant from Romania, arriving at Ellis Island in 1908, and if he were around in 1851, he could be at least 190 years old nowadays."

Johnson pointed up. "And someone at the top is suspicious about his age."

Miller nodded in agreement.

"That would make him the oldest man in the world," said Johnson. "So why are we investigating old people?"

"Besides the 1851 photo, which was recently discovered, there was another piece of information that surfaced a few days ago. Take a look at this security clip." Miller pressed a button on his keyboard. The video clip was in grainy black and white, and it showed what appeared to be a mugging in progress. Then, in the blink of an eye, the robbers flew backward into a dark alley, and the white-haired male victim, who had shoved them, and his companion, a young blonde woman, left the scene in a hurry.

"The NYPD was called by a waitress at the 24-hour café near the incident. She said she had witnessed 'an unusual mutilation attempt' performed by that young woman on the old man. By the time the police arrived, the old man and the young woman were gone. Unaware of what had just happened minutes before their arrival, the police found the two muggers staggering out of the alley, bruised and dazed. The wannabe robbers did not file a complaint with the police, and they split the scene without being questioned.

"A few days later, someone from the private business that owns the surveillance camera saw the video and called the police, who connected the mutilation incident with the video. The waitress recognized the man and the woman as well. Later, Homeland Security identified the old man and the young woman as Vlad Draculesti and Catherina Sanders."

"How can a 190-year-old man be so strong?" Smith wondered out loud.

"Is any man this strong?" asked Miller. "Is he even human?"

"What else could he be?" Smith said. "Is he an alien? ET?"

"Hell, he came from Romania," said Johnson. "Romania, like in Transylvania."

"He's a vampire? Are you serious?" Smith shook his head in disbelief.

"That's what we have to find out," said Miller.

"Why don't we just arrest him and interrogate him?" Smith asked.

"Let's respect a citizen's civil rights for now. We'll monitor him first," answered Miller. "Besides, he may have New York City's best lawyers on retainer."

"And who's the bimbo?" Johnson asked.

"As I said, Homeland Security identified her as Catherina Sanders. She goes by Cat. She could be relevant to his identity or just a young chick trying to dig some money from the old man," said Miller. "All the information I showed you is on your computers and smartphones. Leave no paper trail."

"Who managed to put all this old information together and resuscitate this file?" asked Smith.

"Our computer system. The one with all the data," said Miller, neglecting to tell them about his involvement. "It uses face recognition and when all the lines crossed, it spat out an alert."

"Shouldn't the system worry about terrorists, instead of dirty old men from two centuries ago?" wondered Johnson.

"It's a supercomputer," said Miller, as if that explained it. "Our job is to find out, once and for all, who this Vlad Draculesti is."

"Very well," said Johnson. "Are we authorized to wiretap?"

"We have carte blanche on anything we want to do. Use any department in the NSA you need for surveillance and any additional agents from Homeland Security," said Miller.

"I'll take the surveillance and wiretapping," said Smith.

"Then I'll tail the person of interest and get other resources as needed," said Johnson.

"Good. Report to me via our secure satellite-linked smartphones," said Miller.

"Do we have code names for them?" asked Smith, tilting his head toward the pictures on the screen.

"Vlad Draculesti is Dealer," said Miller, checking his computer. "Cat Sanders is Joker."

"Dealer for the man, Joker for the woman. Fitting," said Smith.

"One more thing before we start," said Miller. "Vlad Draculesti is a very, very rich man. I wouldn't be surprised if he made donations to all the major politicians, regardless of party affiliations, including the president. Tread carefully."

Chapter 2. Cat

My name is Cat, and I am the great-great- . . . great-granddaughter of Vlad V, a vampire. And I am the great-great- . . . great-grandniece of Vlad the Impaler. But I am not a vampire. Until a couple of weeks ago, I didn't know that I – a young professional from New York City – was related to the 15th-century Draculesti family. By now I have somewhat recovered from my shock, and I'm comfortable with the fact that I'm related to Vlad V, a bona fide vampire.

I haven't seen any gory, vampire-blood-sucking activities, nor have I been bitten – yet – since I've met Vlad. I don't intend to be bitten by any vampire, if there are any more of them. According to Vlad, vampires suck a few ounces of blood once a week from their victims for life energy. The blood is not their food. Believe it or not, alcohol is their food, the fuel on which they survive. They must have vampire livers. The biggest surprise of all is that a victim cannot become a vampire, once bitten. To become a vampire, you must be infected by some kind of virus found in the gelatinous blue blood of a strange creature that looks like the devil. Weird!

Vlad doesn't bite at all, luckily for me. He's missing his canine teeth, his fangs. He claims that's why he's getting old, and soon he'll die of old age.

He might be the first vampire to ever die of old age. I'll believe it when it happens. However, Vlad does drink human blood. He claims he gets his weekly drinks from the blood banks. He's never elaborated on how he obtains the blood, nor do I want to know.

And yet, in spite of all Vlad has told me about his bloody and cruel past, I am not afraid or revolted by it. I've started to like my ancient, 560-year-old great-great- . . . great-grandfather, and I feel kind of proud to be his descendant. Not to mention that he may be the closest relative I have nowadays. My parents are dead. They died in a car accident. But since I've met Vlad, a new door in my life seems to have opened. What exactly could this new life be? With Vlad continuing to spring surprises on me, I have no idea how my future will turn out.

Over the past two weeks, I've been spending all my free time with Vlad and learning about the life of a vampire. I should be dating young men, but instead I've been riveted by the stories of an old vampire. Right now, I'm buying my takeout dinner and rushing to see him at his sumptuous apartment on Fifth Avenue. He gave me the code to his place, and by now the doorman knows me and lets me go in just like any other filthy-rich occupant of the building.

Vlad was in his office.

"Hey, Vlad!" I yelled cheerfully as I entered the apartment.

He was on the phone and waved at me. I got the hint and went to the kitchen to eat my dinner. Passing among priceless pieces of art in his apartment made me wonder if the art aficionados knew they even existed. Soon after, he joined me at the kitchen table, dressed in the velvety red robe he uses when he gets out of bed. He is nocturnal, you know.

"How are you doing, Cat?" He brightened up the moment he saw me and gave me a cold kiss on the cheek.

"Great! I've become semi-functional at work. Although I sense that people wonder what's wrong with me and whisper behind my back," I said between bites of sweet and sour pork.

"That's marvelous! Except for the gossiping, which inevitably follows one who suddenly seems to be different." He looked at me with the gratified smile of a grandfather. "I need to discuss a serious matter with you this evening."

"Yeah, like what?"

"Financial matters."

"Yours or mine?" I took a sip from my iced tea. "Mine are nonexistent. I live from paycheck to paycheck." I frowned, sincerely dissatisfied with that aspect of my life.

"Yours and mine." He sat down on the barstool at the kitchen island.

I narrowed my eyes. I had eliminated the possibility of him scamming me for money soon after I met him. Just one of his china plates, from which I was eating my takeout dinner, cost what I made in a day. But the way he said, "yours and mine," made me wonder if he might have marriage on his mind.

He laughed wholeheartedly on seeing my expression. "No, I'm not asking you to join me in a matrimonial union."

How does he do that? It's like he guesses or reads my mind. "That's a relief," I smiled. I really like the guy, but he's my great-grandfather. Why would I think that way? Marriage? What a stupid thought that was! Get a hold of yourself, Cat.

"It is about my financial affairs." He paused and looked at me seriously. "I don't have much time among the living, and my estate is considerable in size. I can give it all to charities or give it to my next of kin. You."

"Me?" My disbelieving laugh died quickly. "But, Vlad, we just met. You cannot leave me your fortune. Besides, you have years to live. You may bury me, for all I know."

He waved away the notion. "Nonsense." He ran his hand over his combed white hair. "You are my blood, from a long time ago. You are the only family that I know of. That's what families do – they take care of each other."

"Vlad, I cannot believe my ears. I don't know what to say." And I really didn't know how to react, either about his proclaimed imminent death or about him making me his heiress.

"I'd much prefer a yes." He smiled warmly.

"O-OK. Let's take it one issue at a time," I said, raising a hand to give me time to clear my thoughts and my throat. "Tell me about you dying."

"Trust me. I don't have much longer to live. I'm sure I won't make it beyond May."

"Are you serious?" I stood up, near tears. "But that's one month away."

"Now, now. We all have to go sooner or later. And for me, it is sooner."

"But, how do you know that?" I started crying.

"Trust me. I do know my end is near." He stood up and took me in his arms. I sobbed uncontrollably on his chest – a very hard chest dressed in dark-red velvet. He leaned his face on my head while he held me.

"I'm sorry," I said after a while. I ran to the bathroom to wash my face.

"Feeling better?" he asked when I returned.

"Not really." I felt like crying again.

"Let's go to the living room. I'll bring some red wine. It will calm you down."

A few minutes later, we were sitting side by side on the oversized sofa, sipping from the Bordeaux he took from the walk-in refrigerated wine cellar near the kitchen – and what a cellar that was!

"I wish we could have known each other a lot longer," he said. He drank from his glass. "But I'm thankful to God that I have met you and gotten to know you."

I stared at him. "Do you believe in God?"

"Yes, sure I do."

"But you're a vampire."

"Vampires are not the children of the devil. I'm a mutated human. My soul desires God, just like yours."

"I'm sorry. I shouldn't have said that." I felt my cheeks getting hot.

"Considering how vampires are described in books and movies, what else would you think? There is a big difference between reality and fiction. There is much more for you to learn about me and the world in general."

More to learn? I nodded dumbly.

"You see, death is not the end," he said calmly. "Just a transition. And I will live in your memory until we meet again."

I wish it were that simple, I thought. But maybe it is that simple. To fortify myself, I took a big drink from my glass. The wine was really good. One bottle probably cost my entire month's wages. I got back to the subject at hand. "How do you know you will die so soon?"

"I know you've felt my body and my hands as being very hard."

"Mm-hmm."

"It wasn't always that way. Yes, as a vampire, my muscle composition is much denser and slightly harder than yours. However, it's never been as hard as my body is now. Eventually, I will become so dense that my internal workings will freeze up and stop functioning."

"Huh?" That made sense in a way. I guess.

"I'm already sensing the end of their workings."

"I guess there is not much I can do about your situation but cry."

"Don't cry, please. You'll need your strength and clear thinking."

"Then what's with all this financial stuff?"

"As I've told you, I've lived for 560 years. Over this period of time, I've made and lost fortunes. However, I accumulated more money than I could ever spend."

"And you want to leave it all to me?"

"Yes. That's the idea."

"I'm not sure that's ethically and morally acceptable."

"Says who?"

"I feel like a gold digger."

"Very well. Let's look at it this way. One day, a Jewish lawyer will knock on your door and tell you that you've inherited a fortune from a long-lost relative. What would you do?"

"Why a Jewish lawyer?"

"Because they've been around longer than me and know their business best, and, besides, my lawyer is Jewish. What would you do?"

"Well!" I scratched my head. "I'm not a fool. I would accept it."

"Voilà! Lucky you! However, in your current situation, you know your long-lost relative. Congratulations! Take the money and enjoy life."

"I feel as if I've won the lottery."

"The DNA lottery."

I felt uncomfortable, thinking about how all this could be happening to me, a business analyst from New York City.

"It's also called an inheritance," said Vlad with a big smile.

"I suppose if I don't like it I can give it away."

"Exactly! Just remember, my dear Cat: When you're rich, it is very easy to become poor. But when you're poor, it is extremely difficult to become rich."

"I won't argue with that." I was a young, idealistic fool. Vlad was pounding some practical sense in my head. "So, what is your plan?"

"Marriage."

Chapter 3. Financial Matters

"What?" I jumped up and curled my hands into fists. I was pissed. I was beyond pissed. And I was feeling sorry for him dying? He was a dirty old pervert. Me, marry him? What was he thinking? What was I thinking even hanging around with him? What a smooth con man. He convinced me that I'm his long-lost great-granddaughter by showing me a portrait of his long-ago wife, who looks just like me. The truth has finally surfaced.

"You – you – you deceived me!" I blurted out, feeling my blood rising to my head. "Telling me that I'm your great-granddaughter! You're a con artist. What do you want? Residency in the US? That's what you want, isn't it?"

"Please calm down, Cat. I am a US citizen. I don't need a green card."

"What kind of sick games are you playing?"

"Would you calm down and let me explain?"

"Why? You lied to me." I began crying. He tried to comfort me and put his arms around me. I pushed him or – better said – pulled myself away.

"I'm sorry. It was very careless of me to tell you upfront what I have in mind by mentioning marriage first."

I calmed down and wiped my tears of anger. "Explain, please."

"It's all about the inheritance tax."

"I don't understand," I said.

"If I make you my heir, after I pass away, you'll pay over half of the estate in taxes."

"So?"

"If we're married, you'll inherit it all without paying a penny in inheritance taxes."

I placed a hand on my hip and the other one on my chest. He was trying to avoid inheritance taxation by using the spouse exemption. "Vlad, I understand now what you're trying to do, but there is a question of morality involved in this." I inhaled to relax and to be able to explain to him why this felt wrong to me. "I believe you, although for a moment I doubted that you were my great-grandfather. I'm sorry."

He nodded and smiled.

"But it feels wrong to me to have a sham marriage with my great-grandfather."

"No one needs to know that we're related."

"But I do. Besides, everyone else would look at me as that bimbo who married the rich old man and now she's inherited his money. Maybe she did him in. You know. I would not have any self-respect. I cannot do what you're proposing."

"Fine. That will be alright by me." He raised his hands in defeat. "You'll inherit my estate as my great-granddaughter."

"I know you want to save the money from taxation, but I hope you understand my feelings about this subject."

"I do. After all, the money will be yours and you have the final say."

"Good." I was relieved that he understood me. Then a thought occurred to me. "Was this a test of my character?"

He chuckled. "Very observant of you. I'm glad you have principles, although I wouldn't have been appalled if you had chosen to marry me and keep all the money."

"How come? Don't you have the same principles?"

"I've been around for centuries, and I've seen very few principled men and no principled institutions. You may think me cynical, but be on guard when you deal with governments, religious institutions, or any other political, economic, or social bodies."

"I don't know what to say. I have faith in humanity."

"Of course. You're young. Just remember what I'm telling you: Most people are noble creatures when you deal with them individually and when no money is involved. The moment two people or more get together and money is at stake, evil joins them. They start with the intention to do good, however it always ends the other way around."

He was giving me sage advice. What he said made sense, as I considered contemporary world affairs.

"I understand your intent about the marriage proposal now. You were trying to deprive government institutions of your money. But I couldn't consider it on moral grounds."

"I am comfortable with whatever decision you make. It is just money." He opened his arms and smiled.

"That's right. Besides, how many millions would be paid in inheritance taxes, anyway?"

"It is good that the financial markets have achieved new heights. I wish the taxes would be only in the millions. However, the inheritance tax will be at least one hundred billion dollars."

Chapter 4. Strigoi

"One hundred billion? Billion with a *b*, right?"

"Yes, billion with a *b*."

That amount was staggering. It was incomprehensible to me what even one billion dollars could do. I could understand ten thousand, even one hundred thousand, maybe even a million dollars. But a billion? It was a number without practical meaning. I stared, emotionless, at Vlad.

"Very well then. I've made an appointment with my estate lawyer, Mr. Abe Yakowitz, for tomorrow morning at 10 am."

"I can't. I'm at work tomorrow," I protested.

"Work?" He looked baffled, and rightfully so.

"I suppose I don't have to worry about work anymore?" I asked meekly.

"There is a big difference between employment and work."

I raised my eyebrows. "What's the difference?"

"Employment is doing something for a paycheck. Work is what every human being enjoys or must do to stay alive. I've never held a job, but I've worked all my life."

"I'm kind of following you," I said, not entirely clear on what he meant.

"After tomorrow, you will have access to funds so vast that you could buy your employer, if you so wished. You can continue being employed, or you could work to manage your new estate."

I felt dizzy about what he was saying. I knew that my employer's valuation was in the nine figures. That amount of money again did not compute. "If you don't mind, I'll keep my job until all this sinks in."

"As you wish," said Vlad. "Therefore, tomorrow morning I'll swing by your building at 9:30 to pick you up and visit Yakowitz's office for us to sign the necessary paperwork. Within a week, you'll have to fly to Geneva and Liechtenstein to acquire the rights to more of my estate held in trusts in Europe."

"Geneva, Switzerland? I don't have a passport."

"Oh, dear! We'll have to expedite one for you tomorrow." Vlad smiled. "After tomorrow, you'll be part of the jet-set."

I nodded. I'd heard about the jet-set type but had no idea what it entailed. Was I supposed to walk around with a poodle under one arm and a glass of champagne in the other hand, while gazing disdainfully at everyone around me, giving

Hollywood kisses to VIPs and calling everyone *darling*? I would soon find out.

The next morning at 9:30 I was waiting at the curb, holding an office box, when a black stretch limousine stopped in front of me. The front passenger door opened, and a man in uniform exited, removed his hat, and said, "Good morning, Miss Cat! My name is Mathew." He opened the rear door for me. "May I take your box?"

Inside the limo sat Vlad, dressed in a dark suit and dark glasses. He invited me in with a gentle gesture of his hand. I handed the cardboard box to Mathew and entered the limo. "Good morning, Vlad!" I gave him a peck on the cheek.

"Good morning, Cat." Vlad scooted to make room for me on the rear bench. "What do you have in that box?"

"Oh, yeah, my box," I turned to look after it as the man in uniform closed the door.

"Don't worry. Mathew will take good care of it. I figured you quit."

"No, they fired me," I said in a huffy voice. "That box contains my personal belongings from my cubicle. I was fired at precisely 8:45 am. The reason: unacceptable performance. For the past two weeks my head's been spinning, so my work suffered, I know, but I was a good employee before I met you. I am pissed the way I was let go. Like a stapler that doesn't work anymore."

"I am sorry about that," said Vlad, a little amused.

"What's so funny?" I was irritated.

"You don't need a job anymore."

"It's just the way it happened. My ego is bruised. I wanted to leave on my own terms." I pouted. "Instead I was thrown out."

"Oh, yes, that's true. But, trust me, by this afternoon, you'll have forgotten all about it." He took my hand and patted it. That made me feel better, although I winced when I felt his hard, cold hands.

It was then that I noticed two gigantic men sitting across from us. One was white, with brown slicked-back hair. The other was black, with a shiny shaved head. Both wore dark glasses.

"Who are they?" I whispered to Vlad.

"Bodyguards," responded Vlad matter-of-factly.

"What? Why?"

"When you reach a certain station in society, you need protection from malcontents and evil characters. Jack and Al are our protection."

I presumed that Jack was the white man and Al the African-American. They sat in their seats like statues, with their massive hands resting on their knees.

"Judging by what I saw a few nights ago, I wouldn't think you need protection," I said.

"I don't. However, should someone try to harm me, it would be imprudent for witnesses to see the villain flying across the street and crashing through a plate-glass window. People would talk and wonder what happened and who I was."

I glanced at the two massive bodyguards. "You have them as a deterrent."

"Yes. Ninety-nine times out of a hundred, people will keep their distance when they see them. Make it a habit to use them."

"Is it that dangerous to be wealthy?"

"Most of the time, no. But it only takes one attempt to ruin your day."

"Are they your employees?"

"No, I contract them when needed. Actually, I have them on retainer."

"From where?"

"From *Bodyguards R Us*." We both started laughing. The two bodyguards sat, unflinching.

"Are they armed?"

"I hope so. In any case, they make a good first line of defense. I have four other, more personal bodyguards who will intervene in case of serious mayhem."

"Really? Where are they?" I looked around, even outside, but I couldn't see anyone else protecting us. "You mean Mathew and the chauffeur?"

"No, they came with the limo. The bodyguards I'm talking about are invisible. They appear when a dire situation arises."

"I don't understand. What are you talking about, Vlad?"

"I might as well tell you now. There are four *Strigoi* that are protecting me," he whispered.

"What are those?"

"Remember when I told you that, after I became a vampire, I returned to Transylvania? I discovered there the lead sarcophagus with the devil's skeleton inside. Well, when I opened the lid, four black, ephemeral entities came out of the box. I sensed them, I felt them, and I was able to communicate with them, in a fashion."

My mouth was hanging open, and Vlad closed it with his hand.

"These creatures, I call them Strigoi – it means ghosts in Romanian. They are not from our world. They were the devil's servants and were entombed in the sarcophagus with the devil."

"What do you mean, not from our world?"

"They are pure dark energy. At most, you would see dark shadows when they move around. Sometimes they screech."

"Did they hurt you?"

"No. They were glad I liberated them from that box, and they swore subservience to me. I became their new master."

"Are they around here?" I turned around and looked.

"I don't know where they are. They appear when needed, no matter where or when I need them."

"Can you summon them?"

"They respond only when anger, fear, or negative thoughts are present."

"From you?"

"Or others. It is uncanny how they appear when they sense villains having murderous thoughts about me."

"Wow! You're not joking, are you?" It sounded too good to be true.

"On my honor, I'm telling you the truth."

"How do you communicate with them?"

"Just through feelings. Speech as we know it is not possible with them, although they facilitate my ability to read thoughts."

"Uh-huh! So you are able to read my mind!"

"Not all your thoughts, just the ones that spike in your mind, the intense thoughts." Vlad saw my puzzled look and continued, "It has to do with the feeling attached to that thought. If what you think does not stir much emotion in you, I cannot detect it. But if you are hungry, let's say, and you eye a delicacy, I know what's on your mind."

"Including anger, pain, or love?"

"Yes, all those and more."

"That's incredible. That is the most potent ability I've ever heard of. You can do everything you want to – persuade, manipulate, coerce and make women fall in love with you."

"It's not that potent. The best thing the Strigoi do is protect me when I'm in trouble. After I pass away, they will serve you."

"What?" I sat up and bumped my head on the low ceiling of the limo. "Ouch!"

"Are you OK?"

"Yes, the ceiling was kind of soft. I will have my own Strigoi?" I asked, patting my head.

"Sure."

"Why didn't they appear the other night, when we were almost mugged?"

"Who says they didn't? How do you think those two punks flew across the alleyway?"

"I thought you did that."

"Yes, I pushed them, and they would have cracked the pavement, but the Strigoi flung them to the hard wall at the end of the alley, where they crashed."

I stared, not totally sure of the implications of having such bodyguards at my disposal.

"And now we have to square away our financial matters. By the way, don't mention to Yakowitz that in three days you'll fly to Geneva and Liechtenstein." He winked at me.

Chapter 5. Heiress

The limo pulled into an underground garage, and we exited into a marble lobby with four elevators. Vlad and I, escorted by our six-foot-four-inch, almost four-hundred-pound bodyguards, took an elevator to the thirty-sixth floor. The elevator's sign indicated that 1,200 pounds was the elevator's maximum capacity, and I'm sure we were near the limit.

A beautiful, gorgeously dressed, blonde paralegal was waiting for us when the doors opened. Compared to her, I felt like Cinderella after cleaning the fireplace and the chimney.

"Good morning, Mr. Draculesti and Miss Sanders," she greeted us in a melodic voice. "I'm Tiffani, and I'll escort you to Mr. Yakowitz's office." She took us to Abe Yakowitz's corner office. And what an office it was, and what a view! A short, bald man stood up from behind his desk and came to greet us.

"Mr. Draculesti! What a pleasure." He smiled, showing his perfect dentures.

"Attorney Yakowitz, how in the hell are you doing?" Vlad grinned and shook his hand. "Allow me to introduce my great-granddaughter, Catherina Sanders. Cat, this is the best estate attorney in the world, Abe Yakowitz."

We shook hands, and I could feel his moist palm.

"Nice to make your acquaintance, Miss Sanders."

"Please call me Cat."

"Please call me Abe." He flashed his pearly whites.

We sat down on the sofas in the seating area adjacent to Abe's ornate desk. Another beautiful, elegantly dressed, but this time brunette secretary came in carrying a tray of silver carafes. She placed them on the coffee table in front of us.

"Mr. Draculesti, may I pour you some vodka?" she asked Vlad.

"You certainly may, Veronica," said Vlad, giving her a big smile.

"What would you like, Miss Cat? Coffee, tea, water, or juice?"

"Water, thank you!" I expected her to ask Abe what he wanted, but she left.

Abe went to his desk and came back with his own coffee mug. "Vlad, what a happy event to find your granddaughter."

I immediately sensed that Abe was not that happy about me being found. Money was the root of his unhappiness, I guessed. A new heiress and new rules worried him.

"Yes, very happy I finally found her," said Vlad. He took a sip of his vodka.

"You never mentioned that you had a great-granddaughter." Abe's eyebrows rose in fake surprise.

"Well, I almost gave up looking for her, when a few days ago, I got the news from a P.I. that he had located her. Miracles happen." Vlad raised his hands to the heavens.

"So, you want to designate Miss Cat as a trustee and the inheritor of your trust," Yakowitz addressed Vlad, who nodded. "I have everything prepared." He turned toward me. "And you, young lady, will be a very rich woman."

"I guess so," I said, somehow embarrassed. Vlad smiled encouragingly at me.

"If you're ready, we can proceed," Yakowitz said.

"Sure." I felt as if I were under water; the voices around me sounded muffled. I wondered if my blood pressure was rising, because I knew that in a few minutes I would be a billionaire.

Abe Yakowitz summoned someone on his phone and, shortly after, a middle-aged woman dressed in business attire entered the office carrying several three-ring binders. Tiffani accompanied her with more folders under her arms.

"This is our associate, Mrs. Lewis," said Yakowitz. "And I think you met Tiffani Arlin."

"Nice to meet you, Miss Sanders," said Mrs. Lewis. "I have the trust books here, and you'll be required to sign your name in each one of them. We will keep two copies, another will be for you, and the last one for Mr. Draculesti. Ready to sign?" She placed the binders on an adjacent standing desk and handed me a fountain pen.

As she pointed, I signed my name many, many times. Tiffani notarized my signature and took my thumbprint.

"Congratulations! You are the new beneficiary of East-West Manhattan Trust," Mrs. Lewis said and handed me one of the binders with my name embossed on the leather cover. "Now, if you allow me, I'll show you the assets and valuations of the trust." She opened my binder to a specific section. "Here are two pages listing the assets of the trust and their valuation as of last quarter." She pointed to a figure at the bottom.

My eyes almost popped out of my head. I read it three times, and I counted the commas to make sure what I was seeing was true. The amount was $147,952,348,299.00 One hundred and forty-seven billion dollars? I was twice as rich as Bill Gates? I was in shock.

"And these are your cards, credit and debit." Tiffani handed me a thin wallet that contained a half-dozen plastic cards. "If you would punch a ten-digit code here to enter your passcode, you'll be all set." She gave me a numerical device pad, on which I entered my favorite ten numbers.

"Congratulations, and it was nice to meet you, Miss Sanders." Mrs. Lewis offered me her hand and squeezed mine firmly. I wish I could have squeezed hers as firmly, but mine was as limp as a banana peel. I shook Tiffani's hand, too.

"I changed the trust into a dynasty trust, Mr. Draculesti," said Abe. "We may be able to avoid a lot of taxes that way."

I had no idea what Abe Yakowitz said, because one hundred and forty-seven billion dollars were bouncing in my head like the balls in a mega lotto drawing. What was a girl to do with all that money? Then an idea hit me.

Chapter 6. Shop 'Til You Drop

"Mr. Yakowitz – I mean, Abe. Can I hire Tiffani and Veronica for a few days?"

Abe Yakowitz looked at me questioningly. "Hire them?"

"Let me explain. I like the way they are dressed, and I was wondering if I can hire them to help me shop for a new wardrobe." I smiled, a bit embarrassed by my shopping desire.

"Oh, I see." Both Abe and Vlad started chuckling. I'm sure I was redder than a Washington apple. "Yes, let's ask them." Abe went to his desk and summoned Tiffani and Veronica, who came in, smiling sweetly. "Ladies, how is our schedule for the next few days?"

Both Tiffani and Veronica searched on their smartphones. "You have a light schedule for the rest of the week, sir," said Veronica. "Golfing after tomorrow."

"Excellent!" said Abe. "How would you like to assist Cat in doing some shopping?"

"That would be so great," said Tiffani, jumping slightly. Veronica's blue eyes widened with delight.

"Well, I won't have to twist anyone's arm then," said Abe. "When would you like to start, Cat?"

I looked at Vlad. "You don't mind if I start by going for lunch with them and then shopping?"

"You're in charge, Cat," said Vlad. "Take the limo and the bodyguards."

"Limo and bodyguards?" said Veronica. "Wow! We're going to do some serious shopping."

I was rich and I needed better apparel. Veronica, Tiffani, and I hit the town, but lunch was first to get better acquainted. Of course, my bodyguards – Jack-Al, as I nicknamed them – became our shadows.

After we were seated in a restaurant, Veronica turned to me. "So, Cat, may I ask you? How did you manage to get Mr. Draculesti as your sugar daddy?"

"He's not my sugar daddy." I felt half-amused and half-upset at the thought. Good thing I did not take the marriage approach. "He's my great-grandfather."

"Oops! I'm sorry." Veronica turned pink. Tiffani snickered quietly, which prompted an annoyed look from Veronica. "It's nice to be a billionaire, I suppose. Tens or hundreds?"

Tiffani wagged her finger, as if to remind Veronica that this was not an appropriate question to ask a firm's client.

Before Veronica was able to apologize, I ignored her question and said, "Yes, I understand, Veronica.

An old rich man and a young chick." I took a sip from my Arnold Palmer. "But tell me, why are you two working for Abe Yakowitz? No, wait. I think I know. Rich future husbands?"

"You're terrible!" exclaimed Veronica, who slapped me lightly on my arm.

"So, I'm right."

"Yes, you are," acknowledged Veronica. "Why not do what all rich folks do? Marry into riches. Except we have only beauty." She repositioned a strand of hair behind her ear.

"Yes, that's one way. Both of you are very attractive, and I bet men are lined up to date you." I winked at them. "Are there any young, rich, eligible bachelors who visit the office?"

"Sadly, no. That department is lacking," Veronica said. "Most are married and old. Life is not perfect. It is a choice between a young, rich husband who's chasing every woman in town, or an older, rich husband who feels as young as the women he beds."

"I guess single old men are chasing young women, too, without intending to marry them," I speculated.

"Nine out of ten," Veronica sighed. "So, what's a girl to do but flirt and give away free samples? But in the end, the whole package will cost," she said, rubbing her thumb and forefinger together.

"Excuse me, but you're not implying that you are prostitutes?" I said, slightly worried.

"Absolutely not!" denied Veronica. "We're not call girls or even escorts. We're looking for husbands, but we don't want to become lifelong mistresses, either. *N'est-ce pas*, Tiffani?"

Tiffani threw Veronica an irritated glance. "Yes, sister. Like you wouldn't throw me under the bus to make *amour* to François."

"You are in love with him, aren't you?" Veronica asked, faking shock.

"Maybe," quipped Tiffani.

"Who's François?" I asked innocently.

"I have to admit that he is the most gorgeous man I have ever laid eyes on," said Veronica.

I could sense Tiffani's jealousy. This François was an object of contempt between the two.

"Yep, George Clooney could not hold a candle to him. And, unfortunately, I sneezed, and Tiffani grabbed him right from under my nose." Veronica took a sip from her iced tea, pouting.

"Is he French? Is he wealthy?" I asked.

"Yes, he's French," said Tiffani. "And he is fabulously wealthy." Tiffani looked away as if longing for him.

"And apparently a super lover," said Veronica.

"How would you know that?" asked Tiffani, slightly annoyed.

"You told me." Veronica shrugged. "Besides, every time he visits New York and you sleep with him, you get these two hickeys on your neck."

I froze. Vampire bites? Vlad told me what real vampire bites looked like. I wondered if Vlad knows about him. "What's his last name?"

"Le Beau, François Le Beau. Do you know him?" Tiffani seemed troubled that I might know him – perhaps intimately.

"No, never met him. Le Beau means 'beautiful' in French, doesn't it?"

"Oh, yes. He is a super hunk," said Veronica.

I laughed, amused by these two and by the super hunk François Le Beau, who most likely was a vampire. A good-looking vampire, apparently.

After lunch, we started at Saks Fifth Avenue. I didn't feel like Cinderella any longer.

That evening, when I visited Vlad, I asked him, "Do you know a François Le Beau?"

Vlad looked at me with those deep, dark, penetrating eyes. "Who told you about him?"

"Veronica and Tiffani."

"That scoundrel," commented Vlad. "He is using Abe Yakowitz as his estate attorney as well. And which of the two did he get involved with?"

"Tiffani."

"Oh, yes. He prefers blondes with green eyes, like those of a cat."

"Is he a vampire?"

"Yes, he is. He'll visit New York soon. You'll get to meet him. But be on guard – he is a playboy."

"Yes, Great-Grandfather. I will be cautious." I patted his arm.

Over the next two days, Tiffani, Veronica, and I shopped at Bergdorf Goodman, Barneys, Neiman Marcus and Lord & Taylor. In between, we hit some small specialty boutiques to complement my "run of the mill" shopping. My apartment was stacked with more clothes and shoes and purses than I had had in my entire life.

I flew to Geneva and then to Liechtenstein, signed more papers, and inherited more billions of euros, gold, bonds, real estate, and God knows what else. At Vlad's insistence, I stopped in Paris and stayed in his apartment on the Île de la Cité with a fantastic view over the Pont Neuf, the rest of Paris, and, of course, the Eiffel Tower.

And I also did more shopping in Paris.

-VVV-

John Miller pulled his phone from his belt holder and read the message. He frowned slightly, and then he read the message to Johnson and Smith, who were standing nearby. "It happened a few days ago, but apparently Joker just became the beneficiary of Dealer's estate. The bimbo hit the jackpot."

"Cat is a fat cat now," said Johnson. "She must give a hell of a blowjob to snatch the old man's money."

"No. Apparently, she is his great-granddaughter, says our informant." Miller finished reading the message.

"Joker is definitely a person of interest now," said Smith.

"Yes. Let's see what develops in this new family relationship," said Miller. "Smith, bug Joker's apartment as well. How are we coming on installing surveillance in Dealer's apartment?"

"Almost there. He uses a mobile phone, no landline. We tapped into it, but nothing of significance. We had to entice the occupants of the apartment below to leave for a few days." Smith winked at Johnson. "Even wealthy people fall for free cruises."

"Good, and you, Johnson, what's this morning report about Dealer?" asked Miller.

"The man rarely leaves his apartment, except in the evening. I have several field agents keeping watch on his moves day and night. I'll request an agent follow Joker from now on. Dealer also stays up most of the night. I used a directional microphone, but the sound is muffled. The windows are insulated."

"Is that so?" wondered Miller.

"Most of the super-rich do that nowadays," said Smith.

"Joker visits him every evening," said Johnson. "She picks up takeout dinner on her way to his apartment. And the old man, I mean Dealer, pays for her cab to take her back to her apartment."

"She never stays overnight with him?" asked Miller.

"Not so far," answered Johnson. "Although I didn't see her visiting him last night."

Chapter 7. Bugs

I returned to New York loaded with more stuff that I had bought in Paris, although I bought less there than in New York, because the prices were – *mon dieu* – steep even for a billionaire. Clearly, my midtown apartment was too small for my lavish new life style. Two weeks ago, I was scraping by, making a living as an analyst working for SWS&S, which stood for the Spruce-them-Wrap-them-Shove-it-down-their-throats-and-Screw-them financial consortium. Now I was part of the crème de la crème. Was this going to my head?

After I arrived back home from Europe, I rushed to see Vlad. I had missed him. He was very cryptic on the phone, so I wondered what was going on. He was waiting for me in the foyer of his apartment and on his forehead he had a yellow sticker that read, "We are bugged." I read it and looked at him with concern. I thought, his apartment has roaches? His computer has bugs? Then I got it: *bugged*, as in tapped.

"Hello, Cat! Welcome back home." He gathered me in his arms and gave me a peck on the side of my head. "Talk generalities," he whispered in my ear.

"I'm so glad to be back, Vlad darling," I said jovially, but in a tired voice. "Europe is wonderful – so many things to see and so exhausting."

"I have something to show you." Vlad produced a CD of classical music. "This is Dinu Lipatti, one of my favorite Romanian pianists, but long, long gone now. Let's listen to him." After the music started, he took me by the hand into his office. "OK, we can talk here. The music covered us coming into my office. The bugs here are muffled, when I want them to be muffled."

"What's going on, Vlad? My God, you look paler than usual. Are you in danger?"

Lipatti was playing a Chopin nocturne in the other room.

"I'm fine, except that, as I mentioned, I'm dying. But let's not dwell on this. Someone in the US intelligence community, either in Homeland Security or the NSA, has gotten wind of my longevity, and they wonder who I really am."

"What does that mean? They know you are a vampire?"

"No, not yet, but they're suspicious." We sat on the sofa in front of Elena's painting. She was so much more beautiful than I. "Director Hoover of the FBI opened a file on me in the 1950s. Soon after, they found my picture from 1908 at Ellis Island. Although I obtained a new birth certificate in 1910 that listed me as the son of Vlad Draculesti, it did not dissuade Hoover from investigating me. Even after he died, they continued. Suspicion about my perpetual youth vanished after I began aging, and they closed the case."

"That's good, isn't it?"

"Almost. My sources tell me – unbelievable as it may seem – that they found a picture from 1851 of me in London."

"Did they have photos back then?"

Vlad nodded. "Homeland Security's supercomputer made the match and sounded an alert about me. Apparently, their programmer did not put a time limit on how far the computer should go back in time." Vlad was thoughtful.

"And you looked the same – your young self – all along?"

Vlad nodded again. "Now, after they put two and two together, they are curious about my physiology. Or something else." His eyes narrowed as he concentrated on some detail known only to him.

"I'm sorry," I said, feeling concern for him.

"Vampires cannot maintain their anonymity anymore. With the advent of photography and more powerful computers, we're doomed." He stood up and paced the floor.

"What are you going to do?"

"Die, which is the easy way out. However . . . "

"Yes."

"If, for any reason, they abduct me while I'm alive or even when I'm dead, they would risk infection when they use a chainsaw to open me up."

"They wouldn't be able to abduct you while you're alive."

"Cat, I'm aging fast, and I'm slowing down. Becoming stiffer every day."

"I'm sorry." I embraced him and leaned my head on his hard chest.

"Me, too. I'm sorry that I don't have more life to spend with you. However, I'm grateful that I found my great-granddaughter, who looks just like my beloved Elena."

I began crying. It was not fair. He was a good vampire.

"Now, now, everything will be OK in the end. Also, your apartment is probably bugged, and our phones and Internet access are tapped."

I sat upright and wiped my tears. "It's that bad? We can't make a move without them knowing about it?"

He nodded. From the other room came the sound of Lipatti's piano. His playing sounded sweet but sad.

"How did you find out about the bugs?"

"I received an anonymous tip."

"Really?"

"Yes, but not necessarily to help me."

"What do you mean?"

"Whoever snitched about the investigation being conducted on me is not my friend. I suspect he has ulterior motives," said Vlad.

"What motives?"

"I don't know yet. I'm sure we'll find out more soon."

"What do we do now?"

"After I was alerted of the intrusion, I inquired with my reliable inside sources, and they confirmed the investigation." He paced around some more. "I had a specialist sweep the apartment and make some counterintelligence changes." He reached in his pocket and handed me a cell phone. "This is a new cell phone. I have one as well. Do not use it in here or in your apartment."

"What's our next move?" I asked.

Chapter 8. Moving In

"Plan and prepare," he said.

"Plan and prepare for your death?" I said, horrified.

"They cannot take me alive. And they cannot have my body." He looked determined. "Come to think of it, the best thing to do right away is for you to move into my apartment."

I couldn't argue with that. It was easier to foil their monitoring while we hunkered down in one place. Besides, his place had a better view. I nodded in agreement.

"I sent for some of my friends to help me," Vlad said.

"I had the impression that you were a loner," I said.

"Yes, but that doesn't mean I don't know people. Better yet, I know vampires just like me."

"Others like you?" Now it was getting serious. He knew others like him, and he would ask the real, fully functioning vampires to come to his aid. And what if one got interested in my blood type? I hoped Vlad would protect me.

"Yes, other vampires like me, but healthier. Don't be afraid – they will not harm you."

He had read my thoughts again. "But will they want to help you?"

"Even if they are not indebted to me, it is in their common interest to pay attention to the new world order. They'll come, although at first I'll ask only my vampire friends for help."

"Vlad, do you have vampire enemies?" I was frightened at the prospect.

"Not many, a few here and there. One cannot help it if over hundreds of years one cannot please everyone."

"Besides me, do you have any other human friends?"

"Acquaintances, business relationships. Not that they know I am a vampire. If I get any human involved, it will be through monetary compensation to perform specific jobs."

"Do you know many of them?"

"I have entire networks set up for all contingencies. But first, you need to move in with me." Lipatti's piano playing stopped.

He motioned with his head to follow him into the living room, which I did. Vlad said for the benefit of the listening ears, "I think you should move into my apartment. If you'd like, I could arrange for all your belongings to be brought here tonight."

"That would be wonderful, darling Vlad." I knew I was a poor actress, because Vlad was speechless, but then he smiled. "But where should I put all my new stuff?"

"How about in this room?" He took me down the hallway to a door, where he entered a code on the keypad next to the door handle. The door opened outward. It was a thick steel vault door. This room was a panic room.

"Brilliant!" I said. "This will do in a pinch." I understood Vlad's plan. The panic room was enclosed in steel plates, and, if bugs were planted in my belongings, communication would not work. "I think I need some fresh air."

We went out on the terrace. The sunset was long gone, but a red band hung on the horizon behind the buildings across Central Park. The wind and the evening traffic noise from down below filled the air. "Why not use the panic room for secret conversations?" I whispered in his ear.

"They may have planted microphones on the steel walls. It is not secure," he whispered back. "I'm happy that you understood why I chose the panic room for your belongings."

"I read mysteries and watch spy movies." I winked at him.

He laughed. "You're a chip off the old, petrified block."

"Well, shall we go and retrieve my things?"

"Why, certainly," he replied.

Listening in on our conversation was almost impossible when we were in an uncontrolled setting, like on public streets. Vlad placed a call for an emergency moving van, and we decided to walk to my apartment. It was late in the evening, and the walk was refreshing after the afternoon rain that had fallen on Manhattan.

"Whatever we do, we cannot alert the IC agents that we know they are listening to us," said Vlad.

"IC?" I asked.

"The intelligence community of the US. They have so many departments nowadays that they fall under one umbrella that goes by the name of IC."

"Thanks. I agree that we cannot let them know that we know. It may come in handy if we lead them astray – give them the impression that we do one thing when instead we do what's needed."

"Now you're thinking, Cat."

"How soon will your friends arrive?"

"Within a day or so. Some may come from overseas."

"And when they are here, where are you going to meet them?"

He paused. "A long time ago, I figured that I could be trapped in my apartment if I were ever discovered. I made certain modifications to the building for quick escape routes and set up duplicate apartments that I could use in case of emergencies."

"Where? In the same building?"

"No. In the two adjacent back buildings joined by common walls. I own an apartment in each."

"You've thought of everything."

"You have to, when you are a vampire. Therefore, my friends will arrive in those safe houses. Meanwhile, I've commissioned a tech team to set up idle conversations between you and me to take place in the Fifth Avenue Apartment."

"I don't understand."

"Those conversations will be played in my apartment to give the impression that we're carrying on with our lives while we assemble in the safe houses – the adjacent apartments."

"Will we be moving into those safe houses?"

"No, it's not necessary at this time."

"How are we going to access the other apartments?" I asked.

"The three buildings have common walls, and the apartments are all on the same floor. As I said, I constructed hidden passages among the three apartments."

"That's so cool! The spies won't know a thing about what we'll really be doing. So what will we be doing?"

"Preparing for my death and for the disposal of my body."

I had to overcome my emotions about him dying. "Disposal?"

"My body is part human, part something else. I am a biohazard. It could contaminate other people if I'm interred or taken to some mortuary to be embalmed. I can end up in some government research institute, and God knows what they'd do with the blue vampire blood. Get my drift?" He winked at me.

I nodded.

"Therefore my body needs to be cremated, or better yet, incinerated into dust."

"How will you do that?"

"I have a lodge in upstate New York, which I've equipped with a military-type incinerator, the same type used to destroy biological weapons. Once I'm dead, my body needs to be taken to that place and incinerated."

"Seriously? And your ashes?"

"I'd like my ashes to be spread in Transylvania, over the town of Sighisoara, from the clock tower there."

"Who would do that?"

"You, if you don't mind." Vlad stopped and looked at me.

"It will be an honor." I embraced him.

"We are being followed," he whispered in my ear.

"Where?"

"Don't look. They're behind us in a black sedan. Although they know about moving your stuff, they must keep track of us at all times."

"All the time? 24/7?"

"Yes," said Vlad and he offered me his arm, which I accepted.

We walked, stepping around the puddles left from that day's rain.

"They must have a big team to do round-the-clock surveillance of us."

"Money is no object to the US intelligence agencies." We walked silently, while Vlad seemed to think. "I wonder why they opened the investigation on me again." He snapped his fingers.

"Maybe the incident outside the café put them back on my trail."

"Are you sure they don't suspect you're a vampire?"

"If they did, they would have sent the SWAT team after me."

"If they did send the SWAT team to arrest you, or even abduct you, what would you do?" I asked.

"If the SWAT team invades my home, I would vanish through one of the secret doors into the other two apartments. I have contingency plans in place for just such emergencies."

"Vlad, what will happen to all your records? There is a ton of information about your life in them."

Chapter 9. The Powerful and the Rich

"Yes, my records contain information that historians would consider a treasure trove. And other interested parties would find it financially rewarding. And, of course, I have a lot of incriminating information against a lot of people in politically and financially powerful positions in the US and abroad."

I gasped but recovered quickly. "I can see the historians' gaining knowledge, but what about the financial stuff and the incriminating evidence?"

"Allow me to explain." He checked his watch as we turned the corner heading down Seventh Avenue. "All people of wealth and importance are engaged in power plays. If they aren't, they will not be wealthy or powerful for long."

"What do you mean, power plays? You make it sound as if there were a conspiracy, as if everyone out there is Machiavellian."

"Well, yes, that's exactly what it is, and everyone must be Machiavellian to remain on top."

"I find that hard to believe. Are there no decent rich people out there?"

"Most of them are decent, however, I'll have to explain in more detail what I mean."

"Please do."

"Take you, for example. You were an employee – you went to your place of employment, performed as well as you could, and tried to succeed by working harder to make more money and climb the corporate ladder. Right?"

"Yes. That's what I did, and would be doing, if I hadn't met you." I squeezed his arm affectionately.

"You made friends, acquaintances, and enemies. You also had a boss and other bosses whom you wanted to impress with your diligent performance. So far so good?"

"Yes, all true."

"Do you really think that every colleague was your friend?"

"I had a few friends."

"Friends who would volunteer to be fired so you could keep your job?"

"Well, no. No one would lose her job for anyone else. That goes without saying." It was obvious that Vlad did not know the realities of office life.

"Do you think that any of your friends would not throw you under the corporate bus, if she had the opportunity for a promotion?"

I had to think about that. "I don't think so. A friend wouldn't do that."

"How many of your friends from work did you talk to after you were fired?"

"Several. Actually, I left text and voice messages, and I sent e-mails."

"Did any of them call you back or reply?"

"None. They're busy. Maybe." I had not thought about it, but this aspect bothered me. Once I didn't work there any more they forgot about me, as if I no longer existed.

"Are they busy? What I'm trying to tell you is that even your work-related friends would conspire against you and everyone else for their own betterment. The reason I asked you about your work friends is because, at work, you were in a competitive environment. All of you competed, and the strongest, smartest, shrewdest – and not to mention, the most Machiavellian – advanced in their careers."

"I see your point. Backstabbing is normal, you say."

"It is in our human nature. When you worked there, all of you played corporate games against each other. If you don't work there any longer, you are not an asset or a threat to them. Your work friends have to concentrate on new relationships, and you're not important anymore."

I stood corrected, and he knew a lot more about the work environment than I did. And these work-friends were my so-called friends? I can imagine what my enemies did or could do.

"You also have friends who are not work-related?" Vlad asked.

"Yes, I have a few. Both women and men."

"Did you tell them about your inheritance?"

"Yes, I did, and they seemed happy at first, but I sensed a certain coldness, even envy, when I told them I was going to Europe."

"It hurts, doesn't it?"

"Yes, it did. It does. I started wondering if there is such a thing as friendship," I said sadly.

"The good news is that there are such people out there to be your friends. True friends are those who are your equals, independent of each other, who share the same interests and values."

"Yeah, you're right."

"It took me one century to figure that out. However, the reason I brought this roundabout subject up is to respond to your comment about power plays and Machiavellianism. While employed, you, your friends, and your enemies were involved in power plays, Machiavellian schemes, to some degree."

"Maybe. But those were benign schemes."

"Sure, because the antes were small. They were for promotions, a few more dollars in your paycheck, better assignments, a nicer cubicle or an office, and so on."

I stopped and looked at him. Damn, he made sense about these facts of life.

"Imagine what people who could lose or gain millions of dollars, or even billions, have to do to maintain or get ahead in life?"

"Sounds tiring." I felt a slight headache coming on. What was I getting into?

"Cat, it sounds tiring because you haven't played those games yet. When you have plenty and want to keep your plenty and acquire more, it all becomes a game. It is a fascinating game, once you get the hang of it."

"And I'll have to do that? It sounds overwhelming."

"It only sounds overwhelming to the people who do not want to try any harder, and you're not one of them."

"Thanks! But, as you know, being a business analyst does not qualify me as the shrewdest and the smartest, not even the hardest working."

"Really? And how did you get your education?"

"I went to college."

"And who supported you?"

"I supported myself in the later years. My parents died, and I had to work many part-time jobs."

"Uh-huh. And you entered university at seventeen, got your degree and MBA in four years – not six years like most – while working to support yourself."

"That's true," I said, feeling proud of my accomplishments. I was only twenty-three years old, and I had been doing well in my professional life before I met Vlad. On the other hand, I regretted not enjoying life during those academic years like other young women did.

"You'll continue to do well," Vlad assured me.

"In other words, I'll have to do what you, and others like you, do."

"Yes."

"That depresses me. It sounds unethical, immoral, and perhaps illegal." God, it was easy to be an analyst and be told what to do. But did I like it? No. It occurred to me that I liked thinking and doing what I wanted to do and not be told by . . . whom? Them? Management? I wanted to be my own boss. And now I was super wealthy, my own boss, and I had to play higher stakes in harder and ethically questionable games. "There seems not to be any justice or fairness in the world," I sighed.

"In my over five centuries of being alive, I have found none. Humans are not capable of attaining nirvana. As for you, just do the best your conscience tells you. You don't have to play the game as I did. You don't have to use the information I gathered on any of the powerful in order to be powerful yourself. But one thing remains the same: Whether you are part of the rich and powerful, or just an employee doing your job, if you appear weak you'll be run over."

I couldn't argue with that at all. It seemed to be the rule from my days in kindergarten to my adult life in the corporate world. The strong dominated the weak. Then a thought occurred to me. "Vlad, you, as a vampire, could rule the world. And I remember you telling me that you, as a prince, were not interested in being a king, but, nevertheless, you could do a lot of good in the world."

"What's on your mind?" he asked.

"You could undermine or sabotage or even kill bad people and tyrants, like a new Hitler."

"And what good will that do?" He gazed into my confused face. "If I interfere and do good for the betterment of humanity, for example . . . let's say, I would have killed Hitler – what do you think would have happened afterward?"

"The end of World War II." I was convinced of that.

"Hardly. Hitler was democratically elected in Germany, and with him dead, another like him would have taken his place. Just like the saying, 'When the student is ready, the teacher appears.' It is the same with leaders: 'When society is ready, the leader will appear.' Good or bad, it doesn't much matter. Or let me give you a different kind of example. The Iranians got rid of the Shah, and who replaced him? Ayatollahs. Are they better off? Depends on who you ask, of course."

"Are you saying that it won't do any good if you interfere?"

"There is no good or bad, just a different outcome," said Vlad.

"Do you mean to say that you could not have prevented the Turks from occupying Wallachia by killing Mehmed II, back in the fifteenth century?"

"I did go after Mehmed II to kill him, to avenge my Elena and my uncle Vlad the Impaler," he said. "I didn't get the chance to kill him. His son Bayezit beat me to it and poisoned him in 1481. And the Ottoman Empire ruled on, even if Mehmed II was dead. Nothing changed."

I exhaled. "The way you describe the world and what people do to each other is terrifying."

"Don't worry, it's a walk in the park for a human. For vampires, it presents another level of difficulty. And you are not a vampire. Yet."

Chapter 10. Blue Blood

I flinched. "Not a vampire yet?"

"That is, if you don't want to be."

"Why would I willingly want to become a vampire?"

"I meant to say that you have that option. You never know what life may throw at you, and that's why I gave you the blue sapphire."

I touched my pendant gem. This was too much at this time to digest. Vlad's immediate situation seemed to take priority now, not preserving my health or wealth.

I returned to my original concern. "Anyway, regarding your records – what will happen if they fall into the wrong hands?"

"Those records are printed on paper. In case of emergency, the records will be destroyed."

"How?"

"The shelves and cabinets are lined with glass, and the paper documents will be soaked in acid. Everything made of carbon will dissolve into a paste."

"But all that information will be lost," I lamented.

"Not the information, only the paper. I digitized all the information, and it is safe. And it is yours to access when you want. Besides, I moved the files into the safe houses."

"Oh, OK. But that information could be dangerous if it falls into the wrong hands."

"Definitely. Take, for example, the vampire blue blood. That stuff could infect any human and transform him or her into a vampire, a superhuman, many times stronger and longer-lived than the average man. The secret of longevity would be very attractive to many, such as a certain Dr. Alfred Hellinherr the Third, to be exact, who would be very eager to find out my secret."

"Who's he? Not a vampire, I gather."

"No, not a vampire. His grandfather, Dr. Hellinherr Sr., an Austrian, found out about vampires and almost obtained an ounce of blue blood. In the name of science, of course."

"But he didn't, I hope."

"No, he didn't. Dr. Albert Hellinherr Sr. wanted to create a serum that could extend people's lives. In reality he wanted to create a super race of soldiers who, in large numbers, could form an army that could conquer the world."

"Oh my God! Another Hitler."

"Hitler was his second choice. He considered him too limited in his thinking. He liked Stalin, who wanted the whole world, and with whom Hellinherr had close ties. Hitler and Stalin financed him equally. Anyway, Dr. Hellinherr Sr. passed his work onto his son, Dr. Hellinherr Jr., who continued the research into finding the fountain of youth. And the son passed the knowledge and information about vampires to his son, Dr. Hellinherr III, the grandson."

"The new generation knows about you?"

"I'm sure they heard of me from Senior. Luckily, Junior and Third don't know what I look like, and the grandfather died long ago."

I looked at him with suspicion, and he noticed.

"Dr. Hellinherr Sr. died of unnatural causes." Vlad paused. "I had to kill him. He knew too much and would have transformed humanity into hell."

Another example of the decisions I may have to make and the deeds I may need to do. And I was involved now. "No wonder you want your body incinerated."

"Now you see? However, even if you think that there could be a super race of vampires dominating the world and subjugating humanity, that would not be the end."

"No?"

"Becoming a vampire is transmitted through blood. Any human can become one if infected. It's similar to contracting HIV, but without dying. Slowly, more and more humans would become vampires. It would get to the point when it would be more desirable to be a vampire than to be a human. As the population of vampires increased, there would be less and less human blood to live on, and, eventually, there would be wars among the vampires to secure humans for their blood.

"Humans would be herded like cattle. Though, on the other hand, any of those human cattle would be a blue blood-drop away from becoming vampires themselves. It is a vicious downward cycle that would lead to the destruction of humanity and vampires as well."

"That is an enormous burden, to keep something like that from happening," I said, feeling the weight of such a task on my shoulders.

"Don't worry. Everything is set up for me to become dust."

We walked in silence for a minute. I peeked behind me and saw the dark sedan following us, annoying the yellow taxicabs with its slow speed.

"You said there are other vampires. How about their blue blood?"

"Good question. You'll meet three of them soon. They are aware of the secret and danger they carry in their veins. They have the responsibility to protect humanity as well. One thing: Vampires are not insane. They are very clear, logical thinkers."

I looked at Vlad for some time, puzzled, as we walked. "May I ask you a personal question, Vlad?"

"Go ahead."

"Why are you so determined to protect humanity?"

"Because the bio-substance that made me a vampire is of another species, not from Earth. It would lead humanity to extinction."

Chapter 11. Fake Chats

We returned with great fanfare to Vlad's apartment, bringing back large trash bags full of expensive rags. We and the helpers dumped them into the panic room. The clothes, dresses, shoes, and purses had lost their appeal to me. Most likely, I would donate them one day and I'd buy new ones, if I felt like it, after Vlad passed away. Knowing that mini-devices *infested* those clothes turned me off them. Vlad had a detector, which confirmed the existence of surveillance bugs in them.

We went out on the terrace to talk.

"I am the principal target," he said softly. "You'll need to go back to your apartment and retrieve a thumb drive."

I raised my eyebrows in surprise.

"The software I told you about is ready for use, and it is on that thumb drive. It's been attached to the back of the toilet tank in the bathroom in the time it took us to return here."

I nodded.

We returned inside.

"Vlad, I need to run to my apartment to get some other stuff I forgot."

"It is rather late," said Vlad.

"I'll get a VIP sedan. So, which bedroom is mine?"

"The corner one." He pointed to its door.

While waiting for the sedan to arrive, I made myself at home in my new, elegant bedroom, which had a four-poster king-sized bed. Not to mention the walk-in closet.

Later that night, I arrived at my old place. The sedan waited for me. I went in and checked my empty apartment. I wasn't sure how many other suspicious people had come in after we left, but at least someone had been to my bathroom to plant the thumb drive in there.

As it happened, I had not brought my toiletries and cosmetics with me. It would seem only natural to return to my apartment, if someone were following me, even at this late hour. I grabbed several plastic shopping bags from the kitchen and went to the bathroom to gather my stuff.

I looked at myself in the mirror. I couldn't believe whom I was seeing now – a different woman. I looked older, too, or maybe tired or more mature. I was rich and playing games that you see in movies. Except this was for real. Was I in danger? It didn't feel that way. Should I run and hide? Not now. I was in too deep. Was I a villain or a victim? I couldn't answer that, and whichever one I was did not bother me. Maybe I was tired. Yes, that was it.

I filled the bags with everything I had in the bathroom and placed them outside the door. I closed the bathroom door and turned off the light. In case they have a camera behind the mirror, they would not be privy to seeing me use the toilet. I sat on the toilet and flushed. While the tank was filling with water, I reached behind it and felt a small object taped there.

I removed it and placed the thumb drive in my bra. I crunched the tape in a ball, which I threw into one of the shopping bags. Mission accomplished. I took one more look at my apartment, and then I left.

On my way to Vlad's place, I sorted through my bags and discarded in a public trash bin all the items that could be bugged. Later, Vlad could not detect any suspicious devices planted in the remaining toiletry items. I had done a good job; I was getting the hang of this cloak-and-dagger game.

Vlad took the thumb drive I brought back and inserted it into a laptop he pulled from a recessed niche near the kitchen. He then connected the laptop to the entertainment center. We talked idly and then went to sleep.

Late the next morning, I made breakfast for both of us, continuing to talk banalities as Vlad had instructed me. He made noises pretending to eat breakfast and complementing me on my culinary skills, which I accepted graciously, although I had only toasted bread and poured cereal into the bowls. Vlad and I read aloud from some nonsense books, as if enjoying some great forgotten literature.

-VVV-

"Joker is back," said Smith.

"Apparently, she finished her work in Europe," said Miller.

"Geneva, Liechtenstein, and Paris," said Johnson. "Financial deals and shopping. Our Interpol connection did not notice any illegal or dubious activities."

"She probably secured more assets from Dealer," said Smith. "What is their game plan?"

"Frankly, I don't see anything out of the ordinary," said Johnson.

"No? How about the fact that they don't have any other friends or acquaintances?" Miller said. "Dealer and Joker keep to themselves."

"Joker contacted some of her ex-co-workers after she was fired from her job, but no one returned her messages," said Smith.

"How about her non-work friends?" Miller asked.

"Nothing there, either," said Smith. "Although we've been monitoring her for only a week."

"Her friends are as plain vanilla as she is," said Johnson. "Nothing of significance, no contact with any suspicious people."

-VVV-

We slept most of the rest of the day. The TV came on automatically so we could pretend that we were watching it. At 6 pm, after we woke up, Vlad put his finger on his lips to ask for silence and flipped a switch on the entertainment center. To my amazement, I heard Vlad and me talking. I sat down to enjoy the show and noticed that speakers in the other rooms came on as if he or I were walking through the apartment, talking about nothing of importance. I understood then all the idle talk and all the reading from the books. The computer recorded us and transferred our voices into its library, using them for the synthetic chatter occurring now.

Vlad turned the faux voices off and said, "Shall we have dinner?"

That evening, I cooked my best spaghetti with sauce out of a jar while chatting constantly with Vlad. His wine complemented my delicious pasta.

Vlad turned on our fake voices and wrote on a piece of paper, *It is time to go to the safe houses.*

Chapter 12. Escape Routes and Safe Houses

Vlad led me to a room on the north side of the apartment. He pointed with two fingers to his eyes and then to one of the ornate walls decorated with bronze flowers in relief, indicating that I pay attention to how he opened that hidden door in the wall. He pulled and turned the second bronze flower from the left in a clockwise direction. He then pulled on it again, and the hidden door opened silently. We entered a small vestibule, and Vlad closed the door behind us. On the right side, he slid open a shield that revealed a security control panel.

"We can talk now," he said. "This vestibule is encased in steel between the two walls of the building. It has a security access panel on the right side here," he pointed to the panel. He knocked on the stainless-steel door we were facing. "Another panel like this is on the other side of this vault door.

"The access is allowed by voice and thumb recognition." He placed his thumb in a slot and a green light flickered. "Open sesame," he said. The steel door unlatched, he pushed it open, and we entered another room.

"Let me set your biometrics so you can have access, and then I'll give you admin access rights as I have." He punched numbers onto the numerical pad, and the blue LED display gave directions on what to do. I put my thumb on the reader and spoke the magic words. "Very well, you now can enter and exit through the secret passages." He then input more codes, and, after I entered my twelve-digit access code, I, too, became an admin for the secret accesses.

"By the way, this is the North Apartment, because you gain access to it through the north side of the Fifth Avenue Apartment's east wall. There is another security access door, just like the one we came through here, between the South and North Apartments. I hope I haven't confused you."

"No, not at all. The Fifth Avenue Apartment is the big place we live in, and this apartment and the other are on its east wall, to the north and south of it. Do you have them coded as such inside here?" I looked around the room for clues.

Vlad smiled at me. "The North and South Apartments are identical in layout but are in mirror image and similarly furnished. However, if you want to know in which of the two we are now, there are clues. What color predominates in this room?"

I looked around and realized that the room had many objects of a dark green color, including the shades on the lamps. The ornate molding on the door was dark green as well. "Green?"

"Yes, this apartment has predominantly green colors, including all the baseboards and crown moldings. I took these colors from the maritime convention: Starboard is green, on your right, as you face the Fifth Avenue Apartment that looks out on Central Park. The South Apartment is the port side, on your left, and it is red – more like a maroon color, actually, which you'll see soon. Clear enough?"

"Then you call them the Red and Green Apartments?"

"Yes. When you're inside them, you don't know which is which except by their color." Vlad place a finger on his lower lip. "However, it is helpful to remember their cardinal locations as well. The Fifth Avenue Apartment building's entrance is from the Avenue and faces west. The accesses for the buildings of these two apartments are from the side streets, one from the north, and the other from the south."

I looked at the room again and realized that it was a bedroom, although it was furnished as a sitting room.

"The beauty of these apartments is that they exit onto two different streets and have different elevators," Vlad said.

"How lucky," I said.

"Not really. I built these two buildings sixty years ago for exactly this purpose, to be safe houses. Right here in this room there is another camouflaged exit to the elevator and stairway, in case of the need for a quick escape." He opened another hidden door, and I took a peek outside into the elevator foyer.

"This door does not have security?" I asked.

"No, it is intended for escaping from here, for getting out. There is no access from the outside in. Shall we continue?"

We walked through the hallway of the five-bedroom Green Apartment. It was green all right; even the countertops in the kitchen and bathrooms were dark-green granite.

"Remember, these two apartments were set up to hide in or, if cornered, to escape from," said Vlad.

"How did you come up with all this stuff?"

"Transylvania."

"Figures! Always have another exit."

"Life teaches you," said Vlad. "I'm giving you a bird's-eye tour of these apartments. By the way, there are more hidden entries and exits in the Fifth Avenue Apartment, which I'll have to show you in silence. And there are the same double walls and hidden accesses in this apartment as well. What I want to show you next is the grand escape route."

Vlad took me to the great room, which contained a large bar. It was centrally located, accessible from the foyer, the kitchen, the formal dining room, and the hallway. And God knows what other hidden accesses it had.

"As you can see, this is the bar," said Vlad.

"Now this is a bar!" It was fully loaded; many commercial bars would fall far short of this one. "Of course, all this booze is your fuel."

"Yes, it is, and I use it as an occasional watering hole. And now, the ultimate escape route." He took me behind the ornate mahogany bar, where there was a supply room equipped with refrigerators, cabinets, and racks full of bar stuff.

Vlad pointed at the quarter round column in the corner. "Now, Cat, pay attention. This quarter round column is all that indicates the shaft containing a descending elevator below and under the street level. Down underground there are many exits to choose from. I'll show you those later as well. You'll need to place your thumb here." He indicated a slot in the thermostat, where I placed my thumb. The round portion of the column swung sideways, revealing a small cylindrical chamber.

"What is this?" I asked.

"It is a secret elevator. It is good for two people. You step inside, release this yellow lever that closes the curved door behind you, and grab this red lever, which will release the brake, and the elevator will descend beneath the street level." He showed me all the levers as he explained the mechanisms to me. "You control the descent speed by how much you pull on the red lever."

"Holy mackerel! But what if you don't have electricity?"

"To descend you don't need power. It has a counterweight. To ascend, you do require electricity, but if there is no power, you use this crank. It's slow but reliable." He pointed to a handle protruding from a metal box.

"Wow!"

"The South or Red Apartment accesses this elevator as well." He pointed to the opposite curved door inside the elevator.

I shook my head in amazement and disbelief. "I've never seen anything like this, even in the movies."

"Of course not – movies are there to entertain you, not to educate you. I gave you the educational tour." Vlad nodded. All he was missing was a pipe to look more professorial.

"Do you expect me to use this escape route?"

"If you need to. You never know when you want to get out or come in here without being noticed. I did this frequently in the sixties and seventies, and we'll have to use these exits again now. Let's continue and familiarize you with the Red Apartment –"

"Oh, my God!" I screamed and pointed. "Th-that bronze statue moved!"

Chapter 13. Mundibuto

"Hello, Mundibuto," Vlad jovially greeted the bronze statue, who was really a shirtless, muscular black man with a shiny shaved head. He was probably six feet tall. The light from the bar, filtered through the multicolored bottles of liquor, cast a bronze-colored tinge on him.

"Mundibuto, this is Cat Sanders, my great-granddaughter. Cat, this is Mundibuto."

"Greetings, massa," Mundibuto said in a deep voice. "Hello, Cat, and nice to meet you. Sorry I gave you a fright."

"Hello, Mundibuto." I moved forward and shook his big hand. "I'm sorry that I confused you with a bronze statue – the light, you know. And you stood still and then you moved your arm, and . . . " I stopped babbling, turned to Vlad, and asked him quietly, "Who's he?"

"Mundibuto is a Negro vampire," said Vlad. "As far as I know the only one in the world. Isn't that true, Mundibuto?"

Mundibuto smiled widely, showing his perfect white teeth. "No need to apologize, Cat. And yes, I'm the only black vampire," he spoke with a Southern accent, puffed his chest, and folded his arms. He looked at his biceps. "Now that you mention it, I do look kind of bronzy in this light. I like it." He walked over to Vlad and they greeted each other by grabbing each other's forearms, like warriors from long ago.

"How are you doing, Mundibuto? Looking healthy," said Vlad.

"How are you doing, massa? You're older than the last time I saw you."

Before Vlad had a chance to respond, I interjected, "Excuse me, Mundibuto, but what are you calling Vlad?"

"Massa," said Mundibuto.

"That's what I thought you called him. Are you his slave and is he your plantation master?" I was incredulous at the notion.

"Yes, he is my master," said Mundibuto. "I don't think he was ever a plantation owner, though."

"Mundibuto, you're going to cause trouble here by using 'massa' when you address me," said Vlad. He turned to Cat. "Mundibuto was my slave for five minutes in 1803. His name back then was Charles."

"Really?"

"You see, I was about to be lynched by some rowdy white folks," said Mundibuto. "Just as they put the rope around my neck, Vlad showed up on his white horse. Yes, he rode a white horse. He happened to have some business in South Carolina, and destiny guided his horse to that crossroads. And he intervened on my behalf and freed me."

"Did you kill anyone?" I asked Vlad, imagining a gunfight.

"No, no. That was my second alternative, if my first one failed," said Vlad with a smirk. "Gold is a great negotiator."

"Yes, he bought me," said Mundibuto proudly.

"So you were a slave owner?" I asked Vlad.

"Yes, but I owned Mundibuto for only five minutes," said Vlad defensively.

"Did you own any other slaves?" I asked him.

"If I did, it was because those were different times. And even back then I did not believe in slavery," Vlad said in a tone that meant he didn't want to talk about the subject.

"Did you keep Mundibuto as your employee?" I asked.

"Very rarely do I keep human employees. I don't want to run the risk of being discovered for who I am," said Vlad. "Mundibuto, being a free man, needed to do what free men do: He took his life into his own hands and didn't depend on a master. In Charleston, I found him a job as a sailor. Seafaring was going to broaden his horizons." Vlad mimicked the hand-over-hand movement of pulling a rope to hoist a ship's sails.

"I still don't understand why you call Vlad massa. You're a free man in a modern world," I said.

"Oh, well, I call him that only when we're alone." Mundibuto looked at his feet. "It is an affectionate name, for me. He saved my life and freed me."

"That's sweet," I said and squeezed his forearm. Boy, was this guy built like a tank or what?

"Well, now," said Vlad. "I told Angelique to take the Red Apartment. I wonder if she has arrived yet."

"I think she's there," said Mundibuto, indicating with his head where I expected the Red Apartment to be located. "By the way, I took that bedroom." He pointed to one of the doors.

Vlad shrugged. He didn't care. There were enough bedrooms in the two apartments to accommodate a football team. "Then let's check on her," said Vlad, adding for Mundibuto's benefit, "I'm showing Cat all the secret passages."

Vlad led the way to the last bedroom in this apartment, and inside the closet he opened another secret door. Using his thumb and the magic words, he opened it, and, to my shock, in the doorframe, stood a naked woman.

Chapter 14. Angelique

I peeked out from behind Vlad, not believing my eyes. I'm sure I blushed, shocked to see a red-haired woman in her late thirties, totally naked, posing with one hand behind her head and the other hand on her hip. She seemed to think nothing of her nakedness.

"Angelique, you look fabulous," said Vlad cheerfully, eyeing her from head to toe.

"Vlad, you look like shit. You're an old fart now," she said in a lively voice and gave him a big hug.

"What can I say?" said Vlad, laughing. He turned sideways between the two of us. "Angelique, this is Cat Sanders, my great-granddaughter. Cat, this is Angelique Brazeau, a woman vampire." He gestured at each one of us with his hand.

"Well, hello, Cat," said Angelique in a slight French accent, looking me over.

"Hello," I said, still embarrassed. I didn't want to make eye contact with her. I didn't want to stare at her tits, although they were in good shape and firm for her age. I didn't want to even glance at her fiery-red bush, which any fireman from the FDNY would have pulled his hose out to quench in a heartbeat. My eyes were shifting from side to side, occasionally resting on her belly button.

"Now, what's the matter?" she asked innocently. "Come here and give Angelique a big hug." Before I could object, she took me in her arms and squeezed me against her firm boobs. She looked at me. "You are such a pretty girl." She grabbed my ass, cupped one of my breasts, and concluded, "And young, too. I bet you make men scream for mercy. Vlad, you should be proud of her." She took me by the hand and pulled me inside the Red – actually maroon and cherry-colored – Apartment.

"How're you doing, you big hunk of ebony?" she asked Mundibuto over her shoulder.

"I prefer onyx. It better describes the hardness of my body." Mundibuto flexed his muscles.

"Uh-huh. I'll have to keep that in mind." She turned back to him and slapped him on the chest as a greeting, and they exchanged a quick kiss.

We walked into the big gathering room of this apartment, and, unlike in the Green Apartment, this one was well-lit. Mundibuto was no longer bronze but a dark ash in color. I suppose that's how pale a black man gets once he's a vampire. Angelique was as white as Vlad, which made her fiery red hair, including the triangle south of her belly button, even redder.

Vlad observed my uneasiness around the naked Angelique and told her, "Have some respect for my great-granddaughter – please put something on."

"Oh, yes." She looked at herself as if just then realizing that she was in her birthday suit. "I'm sorry, dear." She ran into a bedroom to put some clothes on.

"Yeah, I'm embarrassed as well, seeing you in your casual attire," said Mundibuto, and he boomed with laughter.

After a minute, Angelique returned wearing a long, green silk gown. "Better?" She spread her arms to allow for our inspection. It was better, but her nipples were even more provocative from under the silk gown.

"You know I liked you better in your natural color," said Mundibuto, for which he got a scornful glance from her.

"Again, my apologies, dear," Angelique told me. "Now that I've reached this age – over two hundred years old – I'm not as bashful as I used to be when I was human."

"How long have you been a vampire?" I asked innocently.

"About as long as Mundibuto has been a vampire." She noticed my puzzled look. "In 1806, my lover, Maurice the archeologist, dug out a lead sarcophagus in Egypt. I became sick, but I survived and learned how to be a functioning vampire, with

Vlad's help. As it happened, Mundibuto had slept on the crate containing the sarcophagus during the voyage from Alexandria to Cadiz and got infected as well."

I looked at her and then at Vlad, intrigued.

"Vlad helped both Mundibuto and me," said Angelique. "He found out about the dig and came over to the site, where he found me, delirious. He took me with him and, later, he sought out Mundibuto and helped him, too. In a way, we became his disciples."

"Interesting," I said. "And your lover, Maurice?"

"Died. He was older – maybe that was the reason," said Angelique.

"It must have broken your heart," I said, feeling her pain.

"Oh, he was the love of my life. We were together for over twenty years." She looked away as if trying to keep from crying, although I wasn't sure if vampires could cry.

"Sorry, you were his mistress for twenty years? Why didn't he divorce his wife and marry you?"

Angelique smiled. "You are young and modern. Back then, nobility married nobility. Maurice was from a noble family, and he couldn't marry me, a commoner. But I loved him and he loved me, and I decided to choose the next best alternative, becoming his mistress."

The French way, I thought. I was never that much in love with any of my past two full-time boyfriends or my part-time boyfriend. That's why I dumped the part-timer when I found out he was married. I couldn't imagine becoming the other woman in any man's life.

"So, Mundibuto, you still meandering in the African jungles?" Angelique asked.

"Me Tarzan, you Jane." Mundibuto pounded his chest and gave a perfect Tarzan yell.

"It seems the wilderness has sharpened your sense of humor," said Vlad, smiling.

It was an implausible occasion for me to sit down with three vampires. But were they really vampires? That doubt trickled back into my mind.

"You know, Angelique, you look no different than any other red-haired woman out there," I said casually.

"Well, thank you! But what should I look like, except any other red-haired woman?"

"Like a vampire," I said and bit my lower lip.

"Ahh! I see." Angelique exchanged glances with Vlad. "You haven't seen a real vampire yet, have you?" She parted her lips and passed her tongue beneath her upper teeth, which did not look particularly menacing.

I stared at her mouth, imagining her tongue bifurcating.

"Of course you haven't," she continued. "Your great-grandpapa is toothless."

Vlad sighed and Mundibuto got closer to me, as if he were seeing a delicacy in front of him.

Uh-oh! What if I've provoked her, appearing blood-lickingly appetizing? Angelique's irises became slightly red. I didn't want to look at Mundibuto. I would have probably died from fear if he displayed his vampire side.

"Would you like to see a real vampire?" said Angelique. She passed her tongue under her upper teeth again.

"Don't hurt her," pleaded Vlad.

I stole a quick, frightened glance at Vlad, who stood passively nearby with his arms folded.

Angelique got closer to me. I froze.

"I won't harm her," she told Vlad. "She'd better see with whom she is associating. The real vampires."

Her eyes were bloodshot. Blue veins in her forehead began pulsing. She opened her mouth wide and curled her lips back. Her canines lengthened to almost one inch in length. They resembled a feline's fangs of white ivory, gleaming with the wetness of saliva, sharp, and painful. A deep warble sounded in her throat.

I peed myself.

Chapter 15. A Real Vampire

I screamed and ran to the nearest bathroom. I pulled my jeans down and sat on the toilet. My panties were soaked and my pants, too. What a mess! Through the door I heard Vlad arguing with Angelique, while Mundibuto was laughing his head off.

What do I do now? I felt so embarrassed. Wait, what am I embarrassed about? Angelique parades around butt naked without shame, and I freak out when she shows me her vampire face. Even if they know that I peed my pants, I am a human, subject to my feelings and fears. God, she was scary! I shuddered.

I pulled myself together and took the ladylike approach to this embarrassing situation. I cracked open the door and called, "Vlad, may I have a word with you, please?"

He stopped bitching at Angelique, and I heard him coming over to the door. "Cat, I'm sorry. Are you OK in there?"

"I'm fine," I said through the crack in the door. "Listen, I need some, well, some clothes from Angelique." She was about my size, a few extra pounds of lean muscle, but her clothes would do in a pinch. I swallowed. "I need to change."

"Sure," he said. "Angelique, Cat needs –"

"Not so loud, just tell her. It is a woman thing," I told Vlad, rather infuriated.

"Oh! Angelique, would you come over here and talk to Cat, please?"

I heard a small knock on the door. "How are you doing, hon?"

Would you believe that? She called me hon? "Uh, Angelique," I said through the closed door. "I wonder if you have some spare clothes?"

"What did you say? Wait, let me come in." She barged in and I jumped into the bathtub. Her expression of curiosity changed to one of concern. "What's the matter, Cat? Are you all right?"

She was alone with me in the bathroom. The door closed, and I had no escape except down the bathtub drain. I stood slightly stooped, holding my pants up. I hadn't had time to zip them up.

She leaned on the door and folded her arms. "I'm sorry I scared you, hon. I thought you wanted to see a real vampire. Did you wet yourself? Do you need to shower and change?"

I nodded dumbly.

"I'll be right back with a change of clothes." She left.

I was still petrified, in spite of the fact that she was so nice and normal and calm. She called me hon, but God, did she scare me! Seeing her eyes go blood red, the blue veins on her forehead sticking out like varicose veins, her very long and sturdy canines coming out of their sheathing . . . and her mouth wide open, ready to bite into my carotid artery. I shook my head to get rid of that image and the sound coming from her throat.

She knocked and came in. "Look, I understand how you feel. Other people have done worse. But if you want us around you, you might as well know how we look in our vampire form. OK?"

"I guess so," I said, feeling a little less frightened.

"I got you a silk gown, just like mine, except it's red."

"Red?" I said.

"Do you want a white one?" she asked, arching an eyebrow. "Like a virgin ready to be taken by Dracula?" The corners of her mouth tilted upward.

I smiled back. I think I overcame my fear. "This will be fine, thanks. I'll need to take a shower."

"Sure, it will do you good. Here." She placed the gown on the shelf next to the fluffy white towels. "Why don't you get undressed and let me throw your clothes in the washer?"

119

I didn't know what to do at first – undress in front of her? Why not? Cat, stop being a prude, I told myself. I removed my t-shirt, my bra, and my pants together with my panties and gave them to her. My shoes were probably still on the floor of the big room where I had jumped out of them. I pulled the shower curtain and turned the faucet on. Warm water cascaded over my body. It felt good, and it stopped the last of my shakes.

After a half-hour of a good, warm soaking, I turned off the shower and pulled the shower curtain back slightly for a peek. I was alone. Good. I toweled dry and wrapped another towel around my hair. The mirror was slightly fogged, but I could see myself in it. The shower had removed my make up and I, too, looked paler. Like them.

Surprisingly, the medicine cabinet had a complete, plastic-wrapped makeup kit, a set of lipsticks, body lotions, deodorants – including the feminine type – toothbrush and toothpaste, everything a weak-bladdered damsel would need when coming up here for some vampire fun. My hair was dry enough to brush. I applied some light makeup and eyeliner on my eyes. Angelique had bought me only the gown, no panties or bra. So be it. I pulled my new silk gown over my head. Red looked good on me. It complemented my fair skin and sandy blond hair. Angelique knew her colors.

Behind the door I heard them conversing, catching up on vampire news. Should the fair-skinned beauty, in her red silk gown and no underwear, make her entrance now? Might as well, so I opened the door. Vlad, Mundibuto, and Angelique sat relaxed on the sofas, having a drink. When they saw me coming, they halted their conversation, and Vlad and Mundibuto stood up. Vlad smiled in a grandfatherly way. Angelique placed her chin on the knuckles of one hand, admiring me.

Mundibuto licked his lips. "Girl, you look stunning."

"Don't get any ideas," Vlad snarled at Mundibuto.

"What? I'm just admiring her beauty. Like Angelique said, you should be proud of her," he said defensively.

"Good, and let's keep it that way. Look, but don't touch," Vlad added.

"Vlad, darling, I've never seen you so protective before," said Angelique. "It is very charming of you."

"Vlad, charming? That's a new notion," said a man who had just come in through the inner Green Apartment door.

There stood a man who was the handsomest, finest-looking, most gorgeous, attractive, striking, manly, macho, dreamy incarnation of a man I'd ever seen in my life, dead or alive, including angels.

Chapter 16. François Le Beau

"François! Darling!" yelled Angelique. She ran and embraced him. They kissed, too, on the mouth, but no tongue.

"Hey, man!" said Mundibuto, and they gave each other a half-arm grasp.

"Good to see you all. You, too, Vlad." He smiled at Vlad and grabbed his forearm.

François looked at me with his deep, Caribbean-blue eyes, his black hair combed back with only a lock falling on his forehead. He had a square jaw and well- proportioned facial features, and full, dark-red lips. He walked over to me with his hand extended. "And who do we have here?" He grabbed my hand and said, "Hello, I am François. You must be Cat."

"Hello," I said, as if from far away. He raised my hand to his lips and kissed it. I don't think there was a spot on my body without goose bumps. While holding my hand in his, he gently caressed my wrist with his other hand. I felt electricity running through my body. My hair stood up on end, even on my shaved legs. He was divine. His voice was so charming and manly and melodic, and he smelled of good Old Spice. If he continued like this, I would need another shower.

"Nice to meet you, Cat. It is such a pleasure," he said, now caressing my forearm. "Vlad never told me that he had such a beautiful granddaughter."

"Great-granddaughter, you playboy," interrupted Vlad, standing besides us. "Don't get any ideas. New York is full of what you need."

"Now, Vlad, why would you think that of me?" François made such an innocent face, just like the cat that ate the canary. "I was just making my acquaintance with your lovely great-granddaughter."

"Good. Now let her hand go," said Vlad.

François sighed, but, instead of letting my hand go, he took me to a sofa and invited me to sit down. "Can I get you a drink, *mademoiselle*?"

Oh, and he was French, too. "Sure, whatever you're having." I managed to speak in an even tone.

"I'm sure Vlad may have told you that we drink very stiff drinks. It is our fuel." François was smiling at me so sweetly.

"Get her a ginger ale," said Vlad.

I nodded and then said, "Wait, I'll have a glass of Cabernet."

"It will be my pleasure, *mademoiselle*." He walked to the bar so elegantly. I couldn't take my eyes from his cute, black-leather-clad buttocks. He needed to be a model or, better yet, an actor and set new, higher standards for that industry.

And then a thought hit me: He must be gay. He had to be. No heterosexual man looked like him, talked like him, walked like him, and smiled like him. What a tragedy! I moaned.

He handed me my glass of Cabernet. "As you requested, Cat. Can I get you anything else?"

And then I blurted out the question on my mind, "Are you gay?"

He looked at me with his sweet smile and tilted his head, puzzled by the question. He replied, "No, I'm not gay. I'm a vampire. And I prefer women."

Angelique chuckled. "It seems I'm the only one who likes both men and women. *Vive l'égalité!*" She raised her glass and took a long drink.

"I hope I haven't disappointed you, Cat," said François with a smirk.

"No, you haven't," I smiled.

"But you've disappointed me," said Vlad. "I prefer you gay now."

"Me, too," said Mundibuto.

"You?" wondered Angelique.

"Sure. Less competition." Mundibuto exploded into his deep laugh.

"Men!" exclaimed Angelique, looking at me. "Even vampires aren't immune to that kind of thinking."

"Angelique, where do you live now?" asked François, changing the subject.

"Still in Rio, having fun with the young mulatto men and women."

"Why mulattos?" Mundibuto asked.

"Because their blood is so much richer, so much more full of life," said Angelique. "Don't you know that, chasing after the native women in the African jungles?"

"I don't taste any difference between black blood and white blood," said Mundibuto.

"Well, then you'd better visit me in Rio, and you'll find out." She winked at him. "François, I think Cat is curious about how we became vampires. Would you tell her your quick story, darling?"

François came over and sat next to me on the sofa, holding a glass of one-hundred-proof vodka with a touch of Blue Curaçao. "Is this a hobby of yours, Cat?"

"Uh, well, it is all so new to me, and I find it fascinating. And, yes, I'm curious."

"I gather you've heard their stories? Mine is not as dramatic as theirs."

Oh, I loved his French accent. I invited him to continue by leaning forward, closer to him. He smelled so manly.

François looked intently into my eyes. "I was converted into a vampire as part of an experiment."

I thought, Oh, poor darling, he was a victim –

"Because of his own damn fault," said Vlad from across the room, sensing my pity for him.

I straightened up. "What happened, François?"

"You see, I'm not as ancient as Vlad, or as old as Mundibuto and Angelique –"

"Who's old? You're just six years younger than me," objected Angelique.

"I meant since you became a vampire," clarified François. "But shall we continue my story?"

I nodded eagerly.

"You see, I became a vampire through a botched experiment performed on me by the infamous Dr. Albert Hellinherr."

I flinched. Vlad had mentioned something about him, and now he nodded at me as if affirming my thoughts.

François continued, "It was back in 1909. I was a professor of anatomy at the Sorbonne in Paris. In a collegial spirit, I helped Dr. Albert Hellinherr, and I dissected a mummified albino bat from his collection, which infected me."

"So it made you into a vampire?" I asked, feeling my chin tremble.

"No, I became a proto-vampire."

"What's that?"

"There seems to be an intermediate step between a human and a vampire," said Vlad. "Angelique, Mundibuto, and I became vampires because we were exposed to the real vampire blue-gel virus. François, on the other hand, was exposed to some kind of spores or dried blood from the bat, which was a vampire bat – an animal vampire. Afterward, François changed. He was neither human nor a vampire. He didn't develop the vampire canines, although he needed blood to survive."

"Was that bad?" I asked.

"Let him tell you," said Vlad, inclining his head toward François.

"It was bad," he said. "I was dying." He sighed.

"Oh my God, what happened? How did you survive?" I asked.

François took a sip of his drink. "Vlad found me and gave me a choice: die or live as a vampire. I chose to live as a vampire by injecting a drop of

Vlad's blood into my veins. For which I thank you, Vlad."

"You're welcome," said Vlad. "I could have told that whole story in four words: I saved your ass."

Chapter 17. A Shrinking World

"And now, it is our turn to save your *derrière*?" François asked.

"Close enough, but not exactly," said Vlad. "I am dying, not surprisingly, after aging like a normal man. And you all know the cause."

"I'm so sorry, Vlad," said Angelique.

"Me, too," said Mundibuto.

"Same here, old man," said François.

"Well, thank you. I'm moved," Vlad said sarcastically. "I am glad, though, that I've found my great-granddaughter. I never thought I'd find any descendants, and not one as pretty as my Elena." He looked at me with loving eyes. "Anyway, I don't have any regrets, and I don't have much time left."

"How much time do you have?" asked François.

"One month, give or take," said Vlad.

I thought, Oh, God!

"My dying was going to be a simple affair – I die, you cremate me, and Cat goes to Transylvania and spreads my ashes," said Vlad. "Instead, someone in the US intelligence community, possibly Homeland Security or the NSA, opened an investigation on me. I am a person of interest. Cat and I need your help."

"We're glad you called upon us to help you," said Angelique.

Mundibuto nodded.

"Do you know why they opened an investigation on you?" asked François. "Wait, didn't the FBI investigate you from the 1950s to the 1970s?"

"They did, but they came up empty-handed," said Vlad. "They've bugged my apartment on Fifth Avenue, and I've taken countersurveillance measures. These two apartments are clear. However, before I get into how you can help me, I need to talk to you about a troubling future for you vampires."

"Like what?" François asked, furrowing his eyebrows.

"Surveillance cameras," said Mundibuto. "Just as they recently identified the Boston bombing terrorists."

"Yes, however, the investigation on me has nothing to do with that. My case was opened before the terrorist attack," said Vlad. "This is how the situation unfolds for you." Vlad pointed to each of the vampires. "Pictures and videos are captured everywhere, and they end up in a massive database. Homeland Security has a supercomputer that is capable of identifying and categorizing every face in the US or perhaps even in the world. It attaches a serial number to each unique face. The pictures are obtained from the DMV, criminal records, and all the other social media so popular nowadays. Every individual can be tracked by a serial number, face, name, address, Social Security number, DMV records, and, if available, security clearances, employment, fingerprints, and DNA as well. Not to forget political and social affiliations, and international travel destinations. You name it, they can gather it. In short, they are in the process of having a dossier on every person in the USA and on individuals from abroad who travel here."

"Darn, you're right," said Mundibuto. "But Africa is still safe."

"Don't be so sure of that," said Vlad. "People have camera phones in Africa as well. And if the US has started this undertaking, what are the chances that France, the UK, or Brazil are not doing the same thing? What about the whole Western world and China, for that matter? And, Mundibuto, remember, you're an American. So they've got your picture, somewhere. Even if you prefer to frolic in Africa."

"But these measures will reduce the threat of terrorism," I said.

"Of course, and the few civil liberties we have left," said Vlad. "Big brother has, or will shortly have, full knowledge of every citizen."

"I don't see the danger if you are an honest citizen," I said. "Fewer bad things, like the Boston bombings, will happen."

"Perhaps, if you know who the suspects are and what they intend to do," said Vlad. "But just like those two terrorists in Boston, no one had any idea what they were planning to do until the bombs exploded. Yes, they caught them, but they didn't prevent the bombing." Vlad took a drink of Scotch from his glass. "Before we leave this subject about violating our civil liberties – just as I obtained information about the case against me, other, less scrupulous people can obtain information about individuals or groups of individuals and their political inclinations, and their health and wealth status. Businesses already know more and more about us than we do ourselves. All because we already give them the information on Facebook, LinkedIn, Twitter, and any other social and commercial entity that we've done and do business with."

"I agree – we're becoming transparent," said François. "I'm constantly sought out by agents trying to make me an actor. That's why I moved to Montreal. It is becoming more and more dangerous to be a vampire."

"Yes," said Vlad. "You are biohazard entities and biohazard weapons. If these supercomputers identify you for whom you really are – just as they traced me back to 1851 – you may wish you'd die like me."

"No one will take me alive," said Mundibuto.

"Dead will be just fine with them," said Vlad. "And if they take you alive, you'll be their experimental slave."

Mundibuto darkened.

"So what do you suggest?" asked Angelique, visibly worried.

"Even if each of you has different identities, nationalities, and domiciles, eventually you'll be identified. This face identification technology scares me," said Vlad. "How long will it be before they connect the dots about you, François, a good-looking man who many women remember, for good or otherwise? Or you, Angelique, the vivacious woman from Rio de Janeiro? Or you, Mundibuto, the muscular, black monolithic American from Africa?" Vlad raised his eyebrows in perplexity.

"I'd like to be recognized as the handsome one, as well," said Mundibuto, breaking the seriousness of the discussion.

"Well, we live in a shrinking world," said François. "After we take care of your needs, the rest of us will need to contact the other vampires and develop a strategy."

Angelique, Mundibuto, and Vlad nodded in agreement.

"OK, Vlad, what is the plan for you?" asked François.

"Because of this pesky investigation, we'll need to operate from these two apartments, our safe houses," said Vlad. "I have new mobile phones for you. Stop using your own. I'll try to find out who else is suspected in this investigation. Cat is a suspect for sure. I need you to lead them astray while I'm slowly dying. I don't want them to take me hostage, even to get my body after I die."

"And after you die?" asked Angelique.

"Help Cat take my body to a special location to incinerate my corpse. Everything is set up for taking care of my body."

"Why don't you go there until you die?" asked Mundibuto.

I threw him an annoyed look.

"Why didn't you buy a yacht, install a crematorium on it, and enjoy life until the end?" wondered Angelique.

That sounded better.

"Because things got a little complicated," said Vlad. "I have Cat to think of."

"Me? Why?"

"I made you my heiress," said Vlad. "For you to inherit a few pennies after taxes, I need to die properly with an official death certificate, rather than me disappearing, dying, and being cremated in secret. Also, if I disappear, they'll think I'm hiding and will continue to bedevil you, Cat, by searching for me."

"Thanks, Vlad," I said. "If I understand correctly, you intend to die legally and officially."

"Yes."

"I'm afraid I have bad news for you," I said calmly. "Have any of you taken care of someone who has died recently?" They shook their heads. "It's no longer like in the old days, when you died at home, the priest at your side, and they took you to the grave and buried you the next day."

They looked at me, puzzled. They didn't know that dying was a complicated business nowadays.

"Depending on how a person dies, and, in this case, Vlad will pass away from natural causes in his bed, we'll need to call the paramedics or an ambulance, but most likely the paramedics. They could provide your death certificate, if they think you died of natural causes, Vlad. If they're not sure, they'll take you to the morgue, where a coroner could perform an autopsy to determine the cause of death and then issue a death certificate."

They looked at me, astonished at what I was telling them.

"Then the body will be taken to a mortuary of your choice, and they will cremate you, not us."

"Why do they make it so bloody complicated to get rid of the body?" asked Angelique. "Sorry, Vlad."

"Because that's the way it is in the state of New York," I said. "And elsewhere."

"Well, that complicates the matter," said Vlad, standing up. "I didn't know, either, how cumbersome it is. Imagine some coroner trying to cut me open, because for sure the paramedics will not think, after taking a look at my corpse, that I'm even human or died of natural causes."

"What are we going to do? Especially with you being investigated and under surveillance," Angelique asked Vlad, visibly worried.

"I don't know," said Vlad. "We need another plan."

"Yes, we need another plan. Here's what we'll do." They all looked at me, surprised.

"First, as your great-granddaughter, I will need to be the one to make the arrangements with a local mortuary for your fake death. I'll have to do that without them knowing." I tilted my head toward them, somewhere out there. "A mortuary that has a crematorium and can get the job done fast. After you're cremated, the ashes don't talk – they cannot do DNA testing on them, and the investigation is over."

"Good plan," said Vlad, fascinated by the way I took charge.

"I've had some experience in dealing with my parents' funeral. So the question is, after you're dead, is your body going to decay?" I asked.

"I suppose so," said Vlad.

"That means we have to take care of this affair before the real you dies," I told Vlad.

"What do you mean?" Vlad asked.

"We need a body."

Chapter 18. The Plan

"What body?" Vlad and Angelique asked together.

"Another dead man's body, to pretend that Vlad died of natural causes and then cremate him," I said.

"I bet even you couldn't come up with this plan, old man," said François, slapping his knee.

"Well, yes. But we need a dead man," said Vlad.

"That's no problem," said Mundibuto.

"Someone that looks like me," said Vlad.

"I don't see a problem with that, either," said Mundibuto.

"We need someone who's died of natural causes, not drained of blood," said Vlad.

"Again, that's not a problem. An old white man will die of natural causes," insisted Mundibuto.

"Wait a minute," I said. "We don't want you to kill an innocent man. I was thinking about buying or stealing a corpse from the morgue."

"What's wrong with a homeless man?" asked Mundibuto.

I looked askance at him.

"I think we can rustle a nearly dead man who resembles you from an elder care facility," said François to Vlad.

"Please, no killing anyone," I said, trying to make my point. "I'm sure you can get someone who's died recently at the morgue."

"Yes, ma'am. No killing." François gave me a military salute. He was so darling. And if he were in uniform? I didn't even want to think about it.

"OK, OK," agreed Mundibuto, looking disappointed.

"And one more thing: We need a photo identification of the deceased with your name on it," I told Vlad.

"Like a passport?" he asked.

"Yes, or a driver's license. Do you know someone who could fake one and change your picture with the deceased's picture?" I asked.

"I can take care of that," said François.

"I'll look for a corpse," said Mundibuto. "Vlad, can you get me a job at the New York coroner's office?"

"Sure, let me make a few phone calls," said Vlad.

"I'll make the funeral arrangements in Cat's name," said Angelique. She caught my puzzled look. "Hon, if you do it, they'll know our plan. At this time, they don't know Vlad is dying. You keep Vlad company, and I'll impersonate you."

"Oh, good point."

"Also, we will need personal communication devices. I'll get those as well," said Angelique.

"What do I do?" I asked, feeling left out.

"As I said, spend quality time with Vlad," said Angelique. "Act normally. Take walks with him in Central Park. Show them that everything is normal. The most important thing is that you're the mastermind here. Think, keep track of our activities, and let us know the next steps."

"Me?" I was surprised. "OK. We'll text each other via the new phones as we go along."

-VVV-

"This is Dr. Hellinherr."

"Hello, Dr. Hellinherr. I have some information you would be very interested in obtaining."

"Who's this?"

"Let's just say I know a vampire."

"Who's this? Is this a joke?"

"No, this is no joke. I work for the government."

"Are you an informant? I suggest you use the legal channels for whistleblowing."

"I am not an informant and not a whistleblower. I know where you could obtain the blue stuff."

"What blue stuff? I'm not interested in Viagra."

"Not Viagra. Isn't the blue stuff what you call the blue essence of vampires?"

"What is this nonsense? What blue essence?"

"The essence your father searched for all his life, and his father before him."

"How did you get my private cell number?"

"Why haven't you hung up on me yet?"

"What exactly do you want?"

"To sell you something that has eluded your family for a century."

"How do you know that?"

"As I said, I work for the government. I'm connected."

"Uh-huh. What are you proposing?"

"I will send you a cell phone by messenger. We will talk then. But don't delay in calling me. I have other interested parties wanting the blue stuff."

"What is your name? What shall I call you?"

"Miller."

-VVV-

"Hello." It was a woman's pleasant voice.

"This is your dad," said a man. "Any news on the numbers?"

"Yes, I just got the information from her," said the woman.

"How much?"

"Are you sitting down?'

"How much?"

"One hundred and forty seven billion dollars, and change."

The man whistled. "That's a lot of dough."

"Enough for both of us to retire," said the woman. "How much are you going to milk him for?"

"That's a good question," said the man. "And this amount is only what Yakowitz administers here in the US?"

"Yes. I think they have offshore accounts as well. No one knows that information in the office."

"I'll have to think about this," said the man. "This is an incredible amount, and I don't want to leave any cash on the table, if you know what I mean."

"I do. Think big."

"I'll think very big. In the meanwhile, stay friendly with Cat."

"As much as I can."

Chapter 19. Funeral Planning

Vlad and I spent most of our time in the Fifth Avenue Apartment acting normally. During the day we mostly slept. After dark, we ventured outside for walks or to buy groceries for me. We were shadowed at all times. During the night, while pretending to sleep, we made preparations in our headquarters in the South Apartment.

I set up an entire action plan for this undertaking, including milestones that we needed to accomplish. I followed the progress on a spreadsheet and recommended corrective steps if we deviated from the plan or screwed up. So far it was going well, but the difficult part was still ahead of us. Whenever necessary, we held a staff meeting at 11 pm in the Red Apartment to assess our progress.

"What have we accomplished?" I began the meeting.

"I got a job at the NYC Office of the Chief Medical Examiner," said Mundibuto. "In other words, I work for the coroner's office at the morgue, and I handle stiffs all night – fresh or frozen, intact, perforated, slashed, or smashed. Some fried."

"That's good. You got a job there fast," I said, trying to get the picture of fresh, frozen, intact, perforated, slashed, smashed, or fried corpses out of my mind. I may never eat fried chicken again.

"Well, Vlad has connections among people with interest in the dead," said Mundibuto with a smile.

"Did you find my look-alike yet?" asked Vlad.

"There are a few close possibilities in the freezer's body lockers. You know." Mundibuto made a gesture as if pulling a drawer. "But I'm keeping my eye out for a fresh body."

"We don't have much time," said Vlad. "I'm getting stiffer everyday."

"I haven't inspected all the bodies. There are hundreds of them, three or four to a locker drawer, unclaimed. Unfortunately, most are not old, white-haired Caucasians resembling you, Vlad," said Mundibuto.

"White hair won't be a problem. We can dye the hair white," I said.

"I'll keep that in mind," said Mundibuto. "And one more thing, Vlad. You'll need a doctor, if you don't want your fake body to arrive at the coroner to determine the cause of death."

"I'll be the doctor," said François. "I'll be the visiting doctor from Canada."

I wrote another task to be accomplished on my spreadsheet.

"I have a package coming tomorrow at a post office box I set up to receive a fake passport," continued François. "I obtained an entirely new one, but of the old style US passports, with one year to expire and no photo. We will need to take a photo of the deceased, once Mundibuto finds one."

"No problem." Mundibuto folded his arms. "I need to leave soon. I have the graveyard shift. Busy, busy, busy!"

"OK, Mundibuto," François chuckled. "I'll need to take pictures of your eyes, Vlad." He noticed our puzzled expressions. "I'll need to Photoshop your eyes over the picture of the deceased's eyes." Because we still weren't clear on where he was going with this, he explained, "The eyes of a corpse look dead. And by substituting the deceased's eyes with yours, the picture will show you alive and will even resemble you if documents need to be presented after your ashes are scattered."

François was very methodical and professional about this, without a hint of emotion about what we were about to undertake. It seemed as if he had done this before. I love a man with experience.

"You really know what you're doing." I was impressed, and my eyes lingered over his bluer-than-blue eyes.

"I've dealt with corpses and stuff before." François winked at me.

I know I blushed and quickly asked, "Angelique, may I ask why you are a blonde?"

"Because I'm you, honey."

"Oh, OK." What a dumb question. "What are your updates?"

"First, I bought these miniature communicators." Angelique handed each one of us a small plastic package. Inside we found an ear bud, a microphone with a clip-on and a small radio transmitter. "It has six channels – lucky us – one for each of us and a common channel for all of us to communicate and listen. It uses Bluetooth wireless. It is digital and encodes the transmissions, and we piggyback on our cell phones to stay in touch."

"Do we need these?" I wondered.

"Oh, yes! In the heat of the action we need to know about each others' whereabouts," said Angelique. "The other evening when I shadowed your watcher, I could have told you his moves. Trust me – it will come handy. Put them on. Let's try them."

We played with the devices, and they worked great.

"Thanks, Angelique. I don't know what to say. You all are professionals," I said.

"When you're a vampire, you need to learn how to evade or escape the enemy," said Vlad. "If not, the alternative is to kill the enemy, which can get messy sometimes."

Messy? I thought. Like blood splattered on drapes and on walls, blood soaking the carpet, blood flowing like a creek on the pavement? Here was another aspect about being a vampire that had eluded me.

"How about the mortuary, Angelique?" I asked.

"I found the perfect mortuary in Brooklyn," she said. "They do their own cremations. I bought their deluxe package and paid extra for shoving the fake Vlad into the oven first thing when we bring him there."

"We're going to take the body to them?" I asked, not sure if that was possible.

"No, we can't. I've learned that since," said Angelique. "I contracted with a licensed mortuary emergency transportation company to take the body to Brooklyn's Souls of God Funeral Home and Mortuary. And one more thing, Vlad: You are a member of the New Age Eastern Church. According to this religion, your body must be cremated within six hours of the discovery of your death, the sooner the better, such that your soul will not miss its rendezvous with the mother ship."

"What?" Vlad almost jumped.

"That's right, my friend," said Angelique. "I wanted to make you a Jew or a Muslim so your body could be disposed of quickly, but those religions don't allow cremation. You'll have to pretend and become a member of this church. It is a Judean-Islamic-Hindu-Christian fusion religion. You'll fit in there somewhere. Make sure you meet with the holy man when you visit and give him a generous offering, like a check with at least five figures. And get anointed or consecrated."

"All right," Vlad sighed. "Where are they located?"

"Midtown." Angelique handed him a business card. "They have services tomorrow at 12 am."

"At midnight on a Wednesday?"

"Hey, it's a New Age thing. It's hump day." Angelique shrugged. "Go with Cat. Save your souls."

Vlad mumbled something, but we ignored him.

"Angelique, you said the mortuary is in Brooklyn," I said. "We need to be careful about rush hour traffic."

"Since the stiff is already dead, we can do it any time we decide," said Mundibuto, as he was about to leave.

"Except if you get a fresh body, which does not need defrosting," said François.

"Something we'll have to keep in mind," said Mundibuto, and he left for work.

"Where is Homeland Security's base here in Manhattan?" I asked.

"They have a secret Homeland Security center, not far from the UN," Angelique said. "Do you want their address?"

"No. I just wanted to know where they were buzzing from," I said. "If we can, we should leave midafternoon. They'll have to fight the traffic to tail us."

"That makes sense," said Vlad. "But why not rent a helicopter? That will put a kink in their plans."

"Good point," said Angelique. "I'm on it. Then let's do the funeral during the evening rush hour."

Chapter 20. Just a Snack

The next evening, Vlad and I took a walk through Central Park. Angelique shadowed the agent following us and informed us of his movements.

"I hate to break this to you," said Angelique over our common channel. "There are several agents following you tonight. They figured out your routine. And they have directional microphones. I suggest you talk about trivialities."

I raised my eyebrows and looked at Vlad. We talked trivialities.

"You know, the usual agent shadowing you at this time is kind of young and cute," said Angelique in our ears. "I found out that his name is Pratt. I'll take a bite out of him and see how he tastes."

Vlad chuckled. I was mortified. Lucky I was holding Vlad's arm to guide me, otherwise I would have frozen in place. As the path curved, I couldn't help but see the silhouette of a woman approaching a man not far behind us. After a moment of talking, she wrapped her arms around his neck and kissed him, or at least that's what it seemed to me. They stood there in an amorous embrace for a minute or so. I couldn't take my eyes from them. Then, just as suddenly, she let go of him and walked away. The man stood there as if dazed, but then he continued following us as if nothing had happened.

"Is that what I think happened?" I asked Vlad, covering my mouth with my hand so as not to be heard by the directional mics.

"Yes, that's correct," said Vlad.

"Is it that fast?" My curiosity wouldn't let me drop the subject.

"Yes, good enough for a snack." He said it as if he were talking about having a quick bite to eat. "She did an oral extraction, either from inside his lips or from under his tongue. No visible marks, and he may suspect later that he has cold sores in his mouth."

Oral extraction? That means, while kissing him, her canines came out, penetrated a part of his mouth, probably under his tongue, and sucked his blood. His heart was probably pumping it at an increased rate due to the excitement he felt kissing her. My mind went stormy, unable to think of anything else but mental noise.

"Don't worry, no harm done," whispered Vlad, jerking me from my mental dread. "And he won't become a you-know-what. Lucky devil."

-VVV-

"Hello."

"Hello, Dr. Hellinherr. This is Miller."

"What are you proposing?"

"I know a real vampire. What's it worth to you to know his identity?"

"I don't know. Can you give me proof that this person is a real vampire?"

"Let's just say that he hasn't aged since the first picture taken of him in the mid-19th century."

"And you can show me pictures?"

"Yes. I also know that when he was injured he had blue blood."

"Can you give me a sample of his blood?"

"Not without a hefty payment."

"But you are willing to show me his pictures?"

"Yes, because he doesn't look like that anymore."

"How could a real vampire change? He's not a vampire then."

"Oh, yes, he is. He might have had an accident that changed his appearance, but he's the real thing."

"What price did you have in mind?"

"This would be worth a fortune to you, your family, and your institute. I'd say one hundred billion dollars is a fair sum."

"What? Are you out of your mind?" Dr. Hellinherr laughed in disbelief.

"Not at all. You are not the only party interested in vampires, and I will ask him for the same amount."

"Only governments have that kind of money. I'm just a businessman with a few millions, if that much."

"I know. But let's be honest. If you obtained a sample of vampire blood and developed an eternal youth serum, how much would you be worth then?"

"I'll have to think about that. But you must know, I don't have that kind of money."

"Are you interested in a partnership?"

"I'll really have to think about that. Can I call you back?"

"Fair enough. But you cannot call me back. I'll call you in two days, at about the same time."

"Very well, Miller."

"And one more thing."

"Yes?"

"How would you like him delivered? Dead or alive?"

Chapter 21. The Call

When we arrived back in the building's foyer, the doorman said a bicycle messenger had delivered a package for Vlad. Vlad took the manila envelope without concern and thanked the doorman.

Back in the apartment, I started chatting about our refreshing walk. Vlad opened the envelope, after sniffing it for explosives, and pulled a note and a cell phone from it. He read the note and gave it to me. The note said, "I know who you are. If you value your life and your privacy, take this phone into the hallway bathroom, turn on the shower full blast, and call me at 10:45 pm. My number is on the phone's contact list. Be alone, otherwise you'll jeopardize Cat's life."

What the hell? It seemed as if someone knew about Vlad being a vampire. I checked my watch. It was 10:40 pm.

"I'm going to take a long shower," said Vlad, and he stretched. He went to the secret niche, removed the laptop, and entered a few commands. The TV came on, and then I heard my voice saying, "I'll watch TV, Vlad darling." The TV program was about funny videos, and every time the audience laughed, so did my fake voice.

He signaled me to follow him. We entered the hallway bathroom. Vlad turned the shower on –

cold water at full blast – and closed the shower curtain. He whispered in my ear, "Just listen."

He sat on the rim of the tub, near the toilet, and I sat on the closed toilet lid, close enough to hear his phone conversation. At 10:45 pm, Vlad punched the preprogrammed number into the phone. It rang many times.

"Hello." It was a man's voice.

"I'm calling you on the phone you supplied," said Vlad.

"Very prompt of you. Listen, you have a secret that you don't want divulged," said the man on the phone.

"Who is this?" asked Vlad.

"Who I am is irrelevant. What is relevant is that you are a vampire."

Vlad did not respond.

"Hello! Hello, are you there?"

"I'm here," Vlad answered. "What did you say I was?"

"A vampire."

"That is such a silly notion, and this is not even a funny joke." Vlad ended the conversation and smiled at me. He leaned over and said in my ear, "It is not the first time something like this has happened."

My eyes got wide.

The phone rang. Vlad let it ring several times before answering. "Hello."

"Why did you hang up on me? Don't you believe me?"

"Why didn't you call me on my personal cell phone?" Vlad asked.

"Because I don't want this conversation to be heard."

"Heard? By whom?"

"By whomever. Your apartment is bugged and your personal phone is tapped."

"I see," said Vlad. "That's why you asked me to come to this bathroom?"

"Yes." The man sounded irritated. "I hope you're alone in there."

"What if I'm not?"

"Yes, you are. I can hear your granddaughter laughing her head off in front of the TV."

"Interesting. Who bugged my apartment?"

"Me, or somebody else, what difference does it make?"

"What if I tell you that I'm having this conversation recorded, and later on I'll play it outside this bathroom for whomever to listen to your blackmail." Vlad winked at me. He seemed to be having fun, like a cat playing with a mouse.

"You won't do that, if you know what's good for you and Cat."

Vlad narrowed his eyes at the mention of my name and asked coldly, "What do you want?"

"One hundred billion US dollars."

"Are you out of your mind? That is a lot of money." He let out a small chuckle. "What if I don't have that kind of money?"

"Oh, you do. You'll have more than enough, like forty seven billion left over for you and your granddaughter, if she even is your granddaughter," said the man.

"And what do I get in return?" asked Vlad.

"I won't tell a certain Dr. Albert Hellinherr about your secret."

Vlad was quiet.

"Unless he can top the offer, although I doubt that he has that much moolah," said the caller.

"Let me see if I understand you correctly." Vlad checked his watch. "You want me to give you one hundred billion dollars to keep your mouth shut?"

"That's correct."

"If I don't, you'll get the money from Dr. Hellinherr and tell him about me, is that correct?"

"Exactly," said the man.

"If what you say is true about me, and I am a vampire, you know what will happen to you when I find you."

"No need to threaten me. You won't find me and, if you do, I've made sure that, in case of my premature demise, Dr. Hellinherr and other secret entities in the US government will know who you are."

"I'm glad you're cautious. But tell me, didn't we have a similar discussion thirty years ago?"

This time the man at the other end was silent. Vlad checked his watch and smiled.

"I don't know what you're talking about," said the man after a while. "We've never talked before."

"Be that as it may, I need time to think about this," said Vlad.

"No problem. You've got 48 hours. I suggest you don't talk about this in your apartment or with your granddaughter – otherwise, the deal is off the table. And, Mr. Draculesti, make arrangements to have the money ready by the time I call you in two days. At that time, if you say yes, I'll give you my bank account numbers and instructions on where to transfer the money. If you say no, be prepared for the repercussions."

"Understood," said Vlad.

"Good! Be in this bathroom with the shower on two days from now at exactly 10:45 pm." He hung up.

Chapter 22. The Blackmailer

Vlad leaned over and whispered, "Go back to the TV. Ask me about my shower when I return. I'll pretend to be relaxed and to go to sleep. You do the same. Text everyone for an emergency meeting."

Ten minutes later, we gathered in the Red Apartment. Mundibuto was ready to go to work. Angelique had shed her blonde wig and was dressed in her usual silk gown, seemingly satisfied with her earlier "snack." François-the-gorgeous was busy on his laptop.

"A new development just took place," said Vlad. "Mundibuto, you'd better call in sick. We have to have a different approach now."

"That's too bad. I was just beginning to enjoy the morgue," said Mundibuto. "But before you start, I've got something for you." He dragged to the middle of the floor an army-green body bag and unzipped it halfway. A white-haired, shriveled, naked Caucasian man occupied the bag.

I felt my stomach churning. I covered my nose with my hand and turned away.

"He doesn't look like Vlad," said Angelique, inspecting it as if it were a cabbage.

"But he is fresh. Died yesterday of a heart attack," said Mundibuto.

"It looks good to me," said François.

"Not bad," said Vlad. "OK, store it in the meat freezer for now. And come back quickly."

Mundibuto zipped the bag and dragged the corpse to the freezer in the kitchen pantry.

"So, what's going on?" said Mundibuto, rushing back while wiping his hands on his trousers.

"Tonight I've been blackmailed," said Vlad.

"For what?" Angelique asked.

"For being a vampire," replied Vlad. "However, it goes deeper than that. This man is demanding a large sum of money for not divulging to Dr. Hellinherr that I'm a vampire."

"That son of a bitch!" exploded François.

"I don't understand the threat," I said. "Doesn't Dr. Hellinherr know that you are vampires?"

"Yes, his son and grandson know that, however, only Dr. Hellinherr Senior and his daughter Elisa knew Vlad and me personally," said François.

"And we made sure there were no records of us left after we burned down their place in Romania," said Vlad.

"That's when you . . . " I was referring to Vlad's mention of the fact that the doctor had died of unnatural causes. He hadn't said anything about the daughter, Elisa.

Vlad nodded. "Therefore, this blackmailer will identify me to Dr. Hellinherr if I don't pay, not to mention that he threatened Cat."

"He wants to play deadly?" said Angelique, narrowing her eyes.

"Just a threat," said Vlad dismissively.

"Who of the Hellinherrs was the blackmailer referring to?" asked François.

"He wasn't specific, but it must be the Third," said Vlad. "Unfortunately for this blackmailer, I have a very good idea who he is. He tried a similar heist thirty years ago. Somehow he found Nancy, the girl who left me toothless. She was dying in the hospital, and she told him about me being a vampire and how blue blood came from my mouth when she broke my canines.

"He was the last FBI agent who investigated me before they closed the case. He continued investigating me on his own afterward. I returned the favor and ruined his career. He managed to hang onto his job, unfortunately. Tonight I kept him on the phone long enough to track the nearest cell towers. He called from somewhere in Manhattan, near the UN."

"Near the Homeland Security secret offices," said Angelique. "Don't tell me that he works for them?"

"I believe he might," said Vlad. "He is the investigating agent again, and he wants to retire a wealthy man. His name is Tom Brenner."

"We'll have to end him," said François calmly. He looked good even as a potential killer.

"We have no other choice," said Vlad. "He gave me 48 hours – 47 as of now – to decide and to make arrangements for transferring the money into his bank account. He doesn't think I'll refuse. I will not refuse or accept. I'll meet him at 10:45 pm in two days at the location he will be calling me from. Mundibuto will end him."

I winced. I was witnessing a murder being plotted.

"Don't be alarmed, Cat," said Vlad. "He won't suffer. Much."

"But you're planning to kill a man," I said. "A federal agent."

"A dirty federal agent," said Vlad. "Oh, he won't die."

"He'll live happily ever after in the nut house," added Mundibuto, rolling his eyes deliriously.

"What? I don't understand." I was confused.

"Were you scared when I showed you my vampire face?" asked Angelique.

I shuddered.

"Imagine what Mundibuto looks like, especially when he's pissed off and he adds his special voodoo stuff to it," said Angelique, widening her eyes.

"I'll just scare him out of his mind," said Mundibuto, as if he were about to shoo away a crow. "And something else, so you know: I learned in Africa how to put the fear of the devil in anyone's soul."

I was scared. I should have been scared all along. Having a dead body in the freezer, planning to fake the death and cremation of a man – rich or not, I was going to end up in jail. I got the jitters. François offered me a glass of iced tea. I drank it, and I felt better. So much better . . .

Chapter 23. Going Shopping

I woke up the next morning in my bed in the Fifth Avenue Apartment. I was in my cotton nightgown, and I had a terrible hangover. I could barely sit up. The room spun. Then I remembered: the iced tea. Except it hadn't been iced tea, but Long Island Iced Tea, I was sure. They had gotten me drunk to prevent me from interfering.

Someone knocked at my door. "Come in," I said in a gruff voice.

"Good morning, Cat!" Vlad came into the room. He offered me a cup of latte. I turned my head away. "Drink it. It will do you good. It is coffee with Bailey's."

"What? More liquor?" I said indignantly.

Vlad nodded. "Trust me, you'll feel better."

I drank it and liked it. And I felt better in a few minutes. Somehow euphoric and dizzy, but better. I'd become a drunk, just like these alcoholic vampires.

"Who undressed me for bed?"

"You, of course," he said, then he mouthed, "Angelique."

I don't think it mattered, actually. I was becoming a free spirit like Angelique. Soon I'd be walking butt naked in the apartment like her.

"When you feel better, take a shower and come to the kitchen to eat." Vlad left with the empty cup.

By the time I got up, took a long shower, and dressed, it was noon and I was hungry. I smelled garlic and Italian spices coming from the kitchen. Vlad had cooked a ravioli dish; it was the first time I had seen him cook. He saw the surprise on my face and said, "The Food Channel."

After I ate, he turned on the TV and we watched for a minute – what else? – the Food Channel. With a tilt of his head, he invited me to follow him to his office.

"In this apartment, this is the only safe room to talk in right now. Even the terrace is bugged."

"It's that bad?"

"Yesterday, Brenner mentioned exactly the amount in the trust. I called Abe Yakowitz and told him that someone in his office is leaking confidential information about my trust. He freaked out. This could be reason enough for him to be disbarred and even sent to jail."

"Really?"

"Client-attorney information is confidential and severely enforced," said Vlad. "I trust Abe, and he's been my attorney for over thirty years. He will be starting a mini-investigation of his own. However, before he chops heads –"

Meaning he fires a few people – I had to remind myself that's what Vlad meant, because the real and the metaphorical were getting blurry in my mind.

" – I need to ask you, Cat: Have you told anyone about your inheritance amount?" He looked serious.

"No," I said categorically, and I repeated, "No, not to anyone, even my friends, who haven't asked. Except for only one –"

"Who?"

"Veronica Seyler, from Yakowitz's office, asked me in passing how many billions I was worth."

Vlad grabbed his secure cell phone and texted something to someone. He read the instant reply message and then said, "The best thing to do before a war is to have a feast."

"A feast?"

"In your case, shopping."

"You want me to go shopping? Now?" I didn't understand the reason behind his request.

"It will clear your mind. Go out through the other apartment's exit, and I'll let François know that you need his companionship to shop at Rockefeller Center."

"Rockefeller Center? With François?"

At the Green Apartment's entrance, François was waiting for me, with the door to a chauffeured luxury SUV open. He wore dark glasses and looked fabulous. I wore dark glasses as well, just in case someone recognized me. Given the opportunity to hit the town with François, I was wearing a sexy minidress. You know, just in case he wanted to assess my long, beautiful legs.

I stepped into the SUV, and François followed me. I scooted over just to the middle to let him sit closer to me. I felt like a high school girl going out on her first date. François told the driver where to go, and we took off.

"I have a *cadeau*, a gift for you, *mademoiselle*," he said, pulling out of his jacket a small box. He opened it and showed it to me. It was a beautiful platinum cross pendant.

"Ahh! Thank you, François. You shouldn't have."

"It would be my pleasure if you would wear it. It is from Lourdes, and Our Lady of Lourdes will protect you. May I help you put it on?"

"Sure." I turned for him to hang it around my neck and clasp the chain. He touched the nape of my neck ever so slightly, but I was on fire. I made a serious effort not to climb all over him – lovingly, of course. "Thank you!" I managed to say. The pendant was gorgeous and heavy. I loved the way it felt around my neck.

"You are beautiful," said François, and he leaned over and kissed me on the cheek. "Don't mention this to Vlad."

"But he'll see it."

"Not the pendant – the little kiss," he said.

I wished it had been more than a little kiss. He looked heavenly. If it were dark outside, I would have made out with him right there in the back seat. But I behaved. Again.

"The pendant looks nice on you," he said. "Along with your diamond sapphire."

He noticed my other pendant; the one Vlad had given me. It looked like a sapphire mounted inside a marquise-shaped diamond. The diamond was real, but there was no blue stone inside. I wondered if he knew that the blue stuff was vampire blood.

"Thank you! Why are we going shopping at Rockefeller Center?"

"You don't have to shop. Just get out and promenade. Vlad was afraid that you might get cabin fever."

"Yes, that makes sense. Promenade. If I wanted to go shopping, Angelique would be a more suitable companion, don't you think?"

François smiled. Typical man. He wasn't interested in shopping. But then, what?

"Or I could have called Tiffani or Veronica," I said in passing, and I watched him intently.

He turned his head suddenly and stared at me, and then smiled. "I think you are very shrewd and perceptive, contrary to your innocent appearance."

"Little me? Why would you say that?"

"Why did you mention Tiffani and Veronica's names?" He didn't let me respond. "You did it to observe my reaction, didn't you?"

"Maybe," I said.

"All right, here's the deal: We'll shake the tree and see what falls down."

"You mean I'm not the bait?"

"No, I am."

Chapter 24. Confrontation

At Rockefeller Center we strolled through the concourse, looking for nothing in particular. I heard Angelique's voice coming through the common channel ear bud. "She's coming down. Do something innocent."

"Like what?" I asked François.

"Act naturally. It will be better if we stroll diagonally her way." He took my hand in his, and it felt good, although his hand was as cool as the ambient air-conditioned temperature in the concourse.

Just as he said that, one of the elevator doors opened and Tiffani exited. I saw her from the corner of my eye: a tall blonde in a black dress. We walked ahead of her, heading for the exit toward the Summer Garden.

"She's spotted you," said Angelique in the ear bud.

"I see her," said François. "She just put her shades on and then lowered them to make sure it was me she saw."

How could he see her while we were walking ahead of her? He had retro-mirrors on the inside frame of his glasses, I guessed. Spy stuff.

"What the hell!" I said. Outside on the terrace at one of the café's tables sat Veronica with a man in a dark suit. "Why is Veronica here?"

"We presumed that she would be here. But without company," said François. "Change of plans. You deal with Veronica and the man, and I'll face Tiffani."

"Watch out. The blonde seems to be very upset," said Angelique in the ear bud. I'm sure François heard it, too, because he squeezed my hand.

"Ready?" François asked.

"Yes. I wonder who the man is?" Not that Veronica being with a man was unusual, but why here, while Tiffani was conducting business for Yakowitz?

"When we reach her table, if Tiffani doesn't call my name, I'll turn to face her," said François. "You chat with Veronica. It is even better this way."

Then I heard Tiffani calling, "François!"

He turned, faking surprise at seeing Tiffani. I let François's hand go, and I waved at Veronica, who saw us all. The man she was with was tall and slim, with grey-white hair. He looked at me, and, although I couldn't see his eyes because of his dark glasses, he seemed surprised to see me. Did he know me? I'd never met him before.

"Fancy meeting you two together," said Veronica with a sly smile, looking at me and then at François. She wore dark glasses, too. "I didn't know you two knew each other. And look, Tiffani is here, too."

"How's it going, Veronica?" I said.

As she approached us, Tiffani ignored me, but she shot annoyed looks at Veronica and François. "I didn't know you were in town," she said to François.

"*Bon jour*, Tiffani and Veronica. What a surprise. I just arrived for a quick business affair," he lied.

"You don't say? An affair," Veronica said sharply.

Tiffani gave Veronica a murderous glance.

"So you two are together?" Veronica asked me without a trace of embarrassment.

"Well, you know. It's a small world for the jet-set." I smiled at her.

"Excuse me, but I'd like to have a word with you, François." Tiffani reached out and pulled him by the hand a few steps away.

"You and François. Ooh-la-la!" said Veronica, peeping conspiratorially at me over her glasses. "You know this is going to break her heart."

I didn't say a word but observed Tiffani and François.

"You know, it is not my business, but Tiffani's involvement with him could not have ended up any other way," said Veronica. "He's gorgeous and he's rich. And he's a playboy. Too bad." She looked at the two arguing.

I turned toward the table. "Won't you introduce me to your friend?" I asked Veronica, and I noticed her blushing. The man wore an off-the-rack suit and a blue-and-white-striped tie that had seen better days. His dark glasses reminded me of those worn by the Secret Service. He was not a rich man. Was Veronica embarrassed to be caught with him in public?

"Hello." The man stood up and extended his hand. "My name is Miller, John Miller, and I am Veronica's dad."

"Oh yes, dad, this is Cat Sanders," Veronica introduced me.

She and her "dad" sitting at an outdoor café in Rockefeller Plaza in the middle of a workday afternoon? How nice, but I didn't buy it, and I did not have to respond because Tiffani and François were becoming too loud to be ignored.

"You lied to me!" she accused him.

"Cat is just a friend. Calm down," François said. "Let's take a walk and talk." He took her hand. She pulled it away but followed him toward the Channel Gardens.

"Well, it is time for me to go back to work," Miller said. He bent down and gave Veronica a kiss on the cheek. Veronica tensed. "Nice meeting you, Cat." He left before I could respond, his coffee left untouched. Veronica appeared nervous but relieved to see him go.

"Bad luck for Tiffani to run across the two of you," Veronica said to camouflage her sentiments toward Miller.

I sat next to her, pretending to watch François and Tiffani arguing. "It's nice to meet you and your dad on a nice, cool afternoon. Why is your last name Seyler instead of Miller?"

"Long story," she said, indicating that she didn't want to say more.

"You know, François and I are just friends," I said.

"Uh-huh." Veronica was watching the two arguing, but then she turned and looked at me. "Oh, I don't blame you. If I were you, I wouldn't give up the chance to get him in the sack."

"No, we're just friends," I insisted and hoped that my crush on François would not show.

"But he was holding your hand." Veronica looked at me over her glasses.

I felt my cheeks warming up. "Well, I don't know, he offered to escort me on a walk in the city, and, just as we were coming out of the building, he took my hand."

"Ohh! That sounds serious." Veronica raised her eyebrows.

"I'm not sure. I wouldn't want to end up like Tiffani, being jealous and arguing with him every time he's with another woman."

"Hmm. Believe me, you wouldn't want to be Tiffani." Veronica leaned confidentially toward me. "Tiffani is not a poor soul like me. She's from a rich family, but she wants to be independent and not have to associate with them. From what I gathered from talks between us girls, she has an overbearing father. She may have been abused. Maybe she was hoping that she and François could strike up a new life."

If she and Tiffani only knew how hopeless it was to think that François was . . . was what? Not a man, but a vampire. Veronica and Tiffani didn't know that. I felt sorry for both of them. At least Tiffani was financially independent, if she wanted to reconcile with her father. Veronica was just like me before I met Vlad: working-class poor and hoping to find a good man to marry and have kids with, have a nice house in the suburbs, and live happily ever after. Or at least that used to be my dream.

Veronica's small gasp pulled me back from my reverie. François was holding Tiffani's head in both his hands, and he gave her a very long kiss. It was a French kiss, and I had seen it before, one dark evening in Central Park. Afterward, he held her, touching her forehead with his.

"So what if I did?" Tiffani shouted and walked away.

-VVV-

"Hey!"

"Tiffani! What a pleasant surprise. You haven't visited us in a long while."

"I've been busy." Tiffani opened the liquor cabinet and poured herself a double shot of tequila and downed it in one swallow.

"Easy with the booze. What's the matter?"

"I had a rotten day." Tiffany poured another drink. "I quit my job."

"Why?"

"Because I told this bimbo at work how much a certain client was worth, and she leaked the information to someone, and the client found out about it." She downed a second glass and wiped her mouth with the back of her hand. "I had to disappear before trouble engulfed me."

"Hmm. That is bad."

"Not as bad as finding my so-called boyfriend walking hand in hand with this other bimbo who became the same client's heiress."

"I'm sorry. You'll find someone better."

"No, not like François."

"French?"

"No, he's from Canada – Quebec or Montreal, I think."

"I don't know what to tell you. Welcome back home! You can come and work for the family again."

"I don't know. Right now my heart is broken. My ego is battered. I feel like a failure."

"Come back home. You'll feel better. Besides, how great could this François have been? You'll get over him."

"You're right." Tiffani sighed. "At least I won't get hickeys every time I sleep with him. Oops, I shouldn't have told you that."

"Thank you for telling me that detail. I want to know everything about him. I mean everything."

"Go to hell."

Chapter 25. A Night on the Town

Vlad checked the digital recorder to make sure it was set up for a continuous loop of the sound of a running shower. He planned to call Brenner from a location near where Brenner could be while he pretended to be in his hallway bathroom. Satisfied, he said, "We'll leave at about eight and take positions around the calling coordinates. You may want to stay here in the Red Apartment or go back to your bedroom and settle in for the night, Cat."

"Are you sure you need to do this?" I asked with dread in my heart.

"I am certain," he said. "The Fifth Avenue Apartment has the typical fake jabber going on between the two of us. Don't turn it off. We have to give all the appearances of being home so we have an alibi."

"Do you think there will be trouble?" I asked.

"I don't think so. However, one must be prepared for all possibilities, at all times."

Mundibuto, François, and Angelique joined us in the great room of the Red Apartment. All of them wore black outfits, and they had black face masks in their pockets.

"How do we recognize him?" Mundibuto asked.

"I knew him when he was young," said Vlad. "I don't know how he looks now. He's old, near retirement. He could be bald, fat, or slim. The best thing to do is for François, Angelique, and I to triangulate his position. You have the devices, right?"

They nodded.

"Mundibuto will shadow me, and, once I identify him, Mundibuto will give him the African treatment."

"What are you going to do, Cat?" François asked me.

"I don't know. I'll hang around here in the Red Apartment. I cannot go to bed until you're back here."

"Be careful," said Vlad.

I nodded, although my spirits were very low.

They left via the secret elevator without saying another word.

I tried to watch TV, but I was too preoccupied to pay attention to what was on. My cell phone rang and I jumped. It was my old, bugged phone. Should I answer? The display showed Veronica's name. I wondered what she wanted. Better to let her leave a message. Who knows what she may say for the wrong ears to hear?

I waited for a minute and then I called her back from my unbugged cell phone without listening to her message, "Hey, Veronica!"

"Cat? Holy moley, you're calling from a different phone," she said. "Good. Listen, would you like to join me for a drink?"

"I don't know, Veronica. I'm kind of in a bad mood."

"In that case, I called at the right time, girl. How else to lift your spirits but to go out for a drink? Just me and you. Beats TV or needlepoint."

She made me smile. "What the heck, you're right. I need a distraction. Where shall I meet you?"

"Hey, I have an idea. Why not get that fat-ass limo with those beefy bodyguards of yours? We can sample different nightclubs."

That wasn't a bad idea. Having my own transportation would give me a quick escape in case I needed to come back to the apartment in a hurry. "Agreed. Where shall I pick you up?"

"Grand Central. I'll be waiting for you at Madison and 42nd."

"I'll call you when I'm in the limo."

"Sounds good, Cat."

This is just what I needed. I called the limo service and, as luck would have it, Jack-Al were available and would pick me up in an hour. That gave me enough time to freshen up and dress for a night on the town. I went back to the Fifth Avenue Apartment and got ready. Vlad and my faux voices ranted on.

I hesitated. Should I turn the voices off? No, Vlad's voice needed to be heard. But if I leave and they sense that I've left the apartment, they'll know that they've been duped. I must leave by the secret elevator and find my way through the underground parking back to the Fifth Avenue entrance.

The limo pulled in front of me just as I arrived on Fifth Avenue. Very punctual, I thought, and I was sure that the agent keeping watch from across the avenue hadn't seen me. The night was young, and I was going to have a little fun and get my mind off tonight's business. I called Veronica, but her voice mail answered. "Hey, Veronica, the limo is here. I'll see you in a few," I said and turned off the phone.

Mathew, the chauffer tonight, opened the door for me and I stepped in. Jack-Al sat with solemn faces on the seats opposite me. I suddenly became aware of the short skirt I was wearing; I trusted they were professional enough not to drool.

"Good evening, Jack and Al," I said cheerfully.

They nodded once at me, and we took off. Jack touched his earpiece; the blue light flashing indicated a call, probably notifying their dispatcher that they had picked me up.

-VVV-

"She took the bait, sir. We got her," Jack said in a low voice via his Bluetooth.

"Good job," answered a man. "Did you bring the horse tranquilizer, chains, and shackles, like I told you to?"

"They're in the limo's trunk," replied Jack.

"She will be the bait for a bigger prize," said the man. "I'll triple your fee if you capture her old man, Draculesti, as well later tonight."

"Triple our pay? Glad to have the opportunity," answered Jack. "Capture him dead or alive?"

"I prefer him alive. I want to drive a stake through his heart."

"We'll do our best, sir." Jack exchanged a knowing smile with Al.

"Good. Now listen. He will come later tonight to the garage to get the girl. Take him down and tranquilize him. Chain him immediately. An armored truck will come and take him away. One word of caution: He may be old, but he's very strong."

"Not a problem, sir. What should we do with the girl?"

"Kill the bitch and dump her body in the river with a rock around her neck."

Chapter 26. Kidnapped

As Jack ended his conversation, it reminded me that I needed to give them directions. "Wait," I said. "I need to tell the driver where to pick up Veronica."

Jack and Al moved from their seats and sat on either side of me.

"No need to tell him that," said Jack.

"We know where we need to go," said Al.

"How do you know that?" I felt squeezed between the two of them. What was with them, sitting on either side of me? More protection?

"We've received new directions," said Jack.

"What new directions? From Veronica?" How would Veronica know how to contact them? I began to worry.

Jack put his big hand on my upper leg, just below my skirt's hem. "Don't you worry your pretty little head about a thing. Just relax and enjoy the ride."

I tried to push his hand away, but instead he moved it higher up my leg, under my skirt. "Take your hand off me! What's the meaning of this?"

I felt him clamping my leg. To my horror, Al clamped my right leg. I screamed, "Help! Help! Driver, stop the car!"

"Shut up, sugar," said Al. "We were ordered to take you into custody. No one can hear you, and the driver is part of our team. Just as Jack told you, relax and enjoy the ride."

"Oh, crap," I whispered, then more loudly, "Who ordered you to take me into custody? Am I under arrest?"

They didn't answer, but Jack was moving his hand closer to the forbidden zone. "Would you two take your filthy hands off my legs!" I screamed and I hit each one with my elbows. On my left I hit hard beef. On my right I hit Al's holstered gun. Jolts of electricity ran up my arm. I leaned back and blew my hair off my face. I was steamed.

Who were these two creeps? They weren't bodyguards, that's for sure. They can't be federal agents; they don't act that way. They're supposed to be polite and read me my rights, if they were arresting me. And then it dawned on me: Veronica and Brenner. The two were in cahoots. Brenner knew the exact amount in the trust, possibly from Tiffani. But Veronica invited me out. Was Tiffani involved in this as well? Damn, I was being kidnapped!

I knew I was in trouble. Back in the apartment, the fake voices were fooling the real federal agents that we were home. I had managed to avoid the agent on the street. Vlad and the gang were setting a trap for Brenner and knew nothing about my predicament. I was a hostage, and Vlad would not dare touch Brenner once he learned about my situation. This was a major nightmare. What could I do?

I screamed at the top of my lungs.

"If you don't keep quiet, we'll gag you," said Al.

I tried to look up at him, but I couldn't see much past his barrel chest. When I looked to my left I saw Jack's stupid face, licking his lips. Son of a bitch!

It was time to change strategy. I began crying. "Please let me go. I won't tell anyone. Don't you have sisters just like me? Don't you feel sorry for me? I'm an orphan. Please don't hurt me."

"You're asking for that gag, bitch," said Al in a rough voice.

I looked pleadingly at Jack, but the bastard turned away. I guess I was not as enticing with tears running down my cheeks. I inhaled deeply and relaxed. These people were crazy to kidnap the great-granddaughter of a vampire.

"How long have you known Mr. Draculesti?" I asked imperiously, wiping my tears.

They did not respond.

"In case you didn't know, he's a powerful man," I continued. "You two are in for a world of hurt once my great-grandfather finds out about you. I feel sorry for you already."

"You're not giving up, are you, cunt?" Al's eyes were bulging.

Were his eyes bulging from fear or irritation at my attempts to dissuade them from their criminal undertaking? I couldn't tell if I had hit a nerve or not.

"What's Mr. Draculesti gonna do to us?" Jack asked mockingly. "Chew us to death?" They both laughed.

Bastards!

I guess I couldn't use the vampire card. Vlad had no canines, and to them Vlad was an old, feeble, rich man. Wait. These two were after money.

"You know, I'm a rich woman," I said in an assured voice. "I'll double whatever Brenner is paying you."

Chapter 27. Jack-Al

They both tensed up. I could feel their muscles hardening. They both turned slowly toward me. Surprise made them look like two bad boys caught red-handed, except they were not boys but hardened criminals.

"How do you know about Brenner?" Jack swallowed hard.

"Surprise, surprise!" I checked my watch: 10:30 pm.

"How do you know about Brenner, girl?" boomed Al.

"What do you think?" I asked conspiratorially.

"Answer me," commanded Al.

Mathew's voice came over the intercom. "We're here."

"Let's take her in," said Jack. "I'll make her talk."

The limo's door flew open, and Jack grabbed me by the back of the neck and pulled me out. He held me above the ground, just high enough for me to touch the ground with the tips of my toes. I lost my high heels when he dragged me out of the limo. I sunk my nails in his hand to let me go, but he just shook me to get me to stop. I relented, because he could have broken my neck.

"Get her to tell you what she knows," shouted Al from behind us.

"First I want to get my rocks off," said Jack over his shoulder. We were in the underground parking garage. He took me to an office behind a grey steel door. The office had a security wire-mesh window overseeing the garage. He tossed me on the desk and shut the door behind him with his foot.

I lay on my back on the cold, veneered desk. Luckily it was empty. I pulled my skirt down and tried to sit up, but Jack pushed me down. He grabbed my legs from under the knees and pulled me toward him. Without any effort he ripped my panties off and flung them over his shoulder.

He moved his rough hands caressingly from my knees along my thighs toward his waiting pleasure. "Now tell me, sweet thing, how do you know about Brenner?"

I whimpered. I was on a desk on my back, legs spread apart without my panties on, and a brute leaning over me about to rape me, and I couldn't do a thing about it.

"You are a good-looking piece of ass, and you're all mine. I can fuck you gently or fuck you till you bleed. From both holes. So tell me, and I'll be gentle with you. What do you know about Brenner?" Jack unzipped his pants and fished for his wiener.

"OK, I'll talk. J-j-just d-d-don't hurt me." I tried to pull my miniskirt down but he pushed my hand away and leaned over me. "Brenner is trying to blackmail Vlad," I said.

"What?" He straightened up. "You mean he's trying to collect a ransom for kidnapping you. Right?" His bald-headed purple sausage was on the desk, and ever so slightly, I scooted away from him.

"No, Vlad Draculesti is a vampire, and Brenner is trying to extort –" I stopped, wondering if he knew how much Brenner was asking.

"What kind of bullshit is this? Vampire my ass!" He leaned forward, towering over me.

"Wait, how much money was Brenner going to get for me?" I asked him.

"One million."

I started laughing. "You suckers, how about one hundred –"

"One hundred million?" Jack was in shock. His sausage became a hotdog. "Al, come in here."

Al burst in. "You're finished? My turn now?"

"No. The bitch here says that Brenner wants one hundred million for her," said Jack.

"And we were promised a measly three hundred grand?" Al's eyes bulged with indignation.

I'm glad Jack cut me off and I wasn't able to say billions. It would have been as unbelievable to them as Vlad being a vampire.

"But listen to this," said Jack. "It's not for kidnapping her." He motioned with his head back at me. "It's blackmail for not telling whomever that Vlad Draculesti is a vampire."

"A what?" Al asked in the high-pitched voice of a castrated man.

"Vampire!"

"Are you shitting me? There are no vampires, you damn white-ass!" Al started laughing. "Boy, did she take you for a ride!" Al was bent over, laughing hysterically.

Jack turned to face me. By then I had scooted up the desk and pulled down my skirt to cover my privates. He looked like a mad dog, foaming at the mouth. He was going to hurt me bad.

Chapter 28. Waiting

After they had parked their black Yukon Denali a few blocks away, Vlad, Mundibuto, François, and Angelique arrived on foot on 45th Street, between 2nd and 3rd Avenues, at about 9 pm. That location was where the closest coordinates from Brenner's call of two nights ago had been, and chances were that he would be in the same place tonight. They disappeared in the night shadows of the street, while taking notice of seven surveillance cameras installed by different businesses. Those darn things were becoming a modern nuisance for law-abiding vampires.

"How about if we do a preemptive disabling of the surveillance cameras?" asked François.

"How fast will the repair crews arrive to fix them?" asked Mundibuto.

"It could take them anywhere from five minutes to hours," said Vlad. "The street may become too crowded for us to take action. Even the police may arrive."

"Then the next best thing is to fog the lenses of those two cameras." François pointed to two locations on the wall of the buildings.

"Go ahead," said Vlad.

Angelique said over the common channel, "You see across the street, that door down the sidewalk to the left of you, Vlad?"

"I do," said Vlad.

"That could be an exit, not an entrance, from the Homeland Security offices," said Angelique.

"Do you think Brenner will come out of there?" asked Mundibuto.

"Unless he comes out through the front entrance on the avenue. Vlad, when you talked to him last time, was he on the street, in a room, or in a car?" Angelique asked.

"I think he called me from a car," said Vlad. "The voice was softened, and I heard occasional honking, but the sound was diminished, not as if he were outside on the street. Also, from time to time, I could hear the rattle of keys."

"He called from a parked car, then," concluded Angelique. "I wonder if it's parked somewhere on this street."

The time passed slowly. Two men and a woman came out through the secret exit door. They seemed to be taking a stroll and having a smoke. A few minutes later, another smoker, a woman, came out. She did not even wait for the door to close behind her before she lit up.

"This is our chance to make sure if this is the right place," said Angelique on the common channel.

As the woman from the secret exit walked east on 45th, another figure came her way and asked her for a light. The next moment, the two were no longer standing on the sidewalk. A minute later, one of them came out from the shadow of the stairway. She paused and then took a long drag from her cigarette. It must have been good, whatever Angelique had done to her.

"Angelique here," she said on the common channel. "We're waiting in the right place. This is the only back door exit from Homeland Security on this street, allowing for employees to exit for breaks. Other exits are armed and are to be used for emergencies only."

"How did she taste?" asked Mundibuto.

"Too much nicotine," replied Angelique.

"Good work, Angelique," said Vlad, and, before she could thank him, he added, "I'm afraid tonight I'll need all your help."

"What's the matter, massa?" asked Mundibuto.

"My body's stiffening," said Vlad. "I don't think I'll be able to move fast enough to take down Brenner."

"All right then," said François. "Mundibuto and I will take care of Brenner. Angelique will keep watch. I'll approach Brenner –"

"Why not me?" asked Mundibuto.

"I know you love Vlad and would die for him, but –"

"Cut out the bullshit," Mundibuto said.

"Well, Mundibuto, you've spent too much time in Africa. What do you think a white man with a gun will do when approached by a huge black man at night on 45th Street in Manhattan?"

"Got the picture," said Mundibuto. "The bastard will pull his gun on me and then I'll have to kill him."

"That's right, and, remember, he's a federal agent, and he's allowed to shoot you without fear of ending up in jail," said François.

"Would you two cut the chat!" said Angelique. "What's the plan, Vlad?"

"Thank you, Angelique, for taking care of the youngsters!" said Vlad. "I don't know what Brenner will do. However, he may go to his car again. Whichever door he chooses to get into his car, François, you get in with him on that side, Mundibuto on the other side, sandwiching him, and I'll get in after you for a chat."

"Provided he doesn't have one of those environmentally friendly cars, where only two men and a boy can squeeze in," said Mundibuto.

"Then Brenner will be the boy," replied Vlad. "Angelique, please keep watch –"

"*Merde*! Shit!" interrupted François. "Cat is on the move."

"I told her to stay home," Vlad sighed.

"She's moving south on Fifth Avenue," said François.

"Maybe she decided to take a walk, get some fresh air," speculated Angelique.

"No, she's not walking," François said. "The motion indicates she's in a vehicle."

"In a taxi?" Angelique wondered.

"I told Cat not to venture outside without an escort," said Vlad.

"Maybe she's following your instructions," said Angelique.

Vlad thought for a moment, and then he spotted a man coming out of the Homeland Security secret exit and recognized him. "That's Brenner."

Chapter 29. The Bagging

"We see him," said the other three vampires.

A tall, gray-haired man, dressed in a dark suit and striped tie, stood on the sidewalk, sniffing the night air.

"Vlad, he looks a bit like you," said Angelique.

"We senior citizens all look alike," said Vlad. "Change of plans. François, find Cat."

"I'm on it," said François.

"Angelique, you'll take François's place. Let's deal with this son of a bitch." Vlad was pissed and worried about Cat.

"He's walking toward that fat-ass sedan near you, Vlad," said Angelique.

Brenner went around the large Crown Victoria and approached the Toyota Prius parked in front of it. He leaned on the Prius's door, inspecting the surroundings while lighting a cigarette. Vlad stood in the shadow of the building right across from the Prius.

"I'll be!" whispered Vlad. "An environmentally conscious dirty agent."

"He's early," said Mundibuto.

"Get ready," said Vlad. "The Prius has a keyless entry."

"I'm behind the car," said Angelique.

Just as she said that, a NYPD patrol car passed by, doing its rounds. Brenner observed the patrol car while puffing on his cigarette. After the patrol car passed Third Avenue, Brenner turned on his phone and checked his messages. The cigarette glowed as he inhaled, revealing a satisfied smile on his face.

"OK, Dracula, I know you're out here," said Brenner. "Come on out."

Vlad glanced at the cell phone Brenner had provided him. It was bugged. Brenner tracked the location of the phone and knew Vlad's location. "Angelique and Mundibuto, get ready to strip him naked, in case he's wired, and bag him," said Vlad softly. "I'll talk to him, but I'll stay in the shadow."

Brenner looked right at the shadow where Vlad was hiding. "In case you want to do something foolish, I've got Cat, and they are in a safe location."

"What?" said Vlad, alarmed from his shadowy place.

"That's right," said Brenner. "Insurance and extra motivation for you to do as I tell you."

"So you're not in this by yourself?" asked Vlad.

"No, of course not. I have accomplices." Brenner laughed. "Don't be foolish, Dracula. You have only one chance to save Cat, and you have an hour to transfer the amount I demanded. I'll text you the account numbers shortly."

Just as he finished saying that, Vlad called, "Get him!"

Brenner disappeared, pulled down in the gutter by his ankles. He had no time to pull out his sidearm, say a word, or even scream before Angelique knocked him out cold. Mundibuto crawled along the gutter and pulled his clothes off him as if he were peeling a banana. Very little of Brenner's white flesh was visible as Mundibuto stripped him and at the same time shoved him into the dark-green body bag.

"He was wired," said Mundibuto. "He's naked and clean now."

Vlad clasped the handle of the Prius, but the door did not unlatch. It was not Brenner's car, and the remote opener was in his clothes in the gutter. He skittered to it and gave the clothes a quick check. The remote was for the Ford Crown Victoria, his government-issued car. "Use his car, the Crown Victoria, and take him to the Denali," Vlad said, as he tossed the keys to Angelique. "I'll meet you there in a short while." In the clothes' pockets he found Brenner's wallet, security ID badge, gun, the phone, and the wire. He turned off the wire's transmission, pulled out the phone's battery, and placed them in his pocket, along with the wallet. He opened a black plastic bag and shoved the clothes in it, along with the gun. Scurrying along the gutter and keeping out of the range of the surveillance cameras, Vlad ran down Second Avenue to 42st Street, where he turned to run toward the East River. On the way he found a chunk of concrete, which he placed in the bag. He squeezed the air out of the bag, made small punctures in it, and tied the bag shut with a knot. Near the FDR Drive, from under the shadows of the trees, he hurled the bag containing the clothes, gun, and the concrete chunk into the river.

Inside the Denali, Mundibuto wrapped Agent Brenner in clear plastic like a cocoon for easy handling and shipping. He sealed his eyes and mouth with duct tape. Mundibuto put him back in the bag in a sitting position with just his head showing and strapped him into the middle seat. Angelique and Mundibuto sat on either side of him. Brenner came out of his mild concussion but couldn't utter a word because of the duct tape on his mouth. He made muffled sounds as he struggled in vain to free himself.

Vlad arrived at the SUV and got into the front passenger seat. He consulted his watch and then made a sign to Mundibuto to peel the duct tape off his mouth. Brenner gave a cry of pain as the tape came off at lightning speed.

"So, Agent Brenner, according to your security ID card here, your name is John Miller. Can you explain why your name is different?" asked Vlad.

"Go fuck yourself. And in case you don't realize this, kidnapping a federal agent is a capital offense."

"I hope so. You kidnapped Cat. Where did you take her?"

"If you don't let me go immediately and my associates don't hear from me within a minute, Cat is as good as dead," said Brenner, or Miller, or whoever he was.

"Good point." Vlad inserted the battery back into Brenner's phone and checked the contact list. "This is the last time I'm asking you: Where is Cat?"

"Don't you value Cat's – holy shit!" Brenner screamed from the pain when Mundibuto pulled the duct tape off his eyes, along with most of his eyebrows and eyelashes. Brenner looked around, bewildered. He glanced at Angelique and Mundibuto, and then looked down at the body bag he was stuffed in. "What's the meaning of this, Mr. Draculesti?" he asked Vlad.

"In case we have to kill you, you're already in a body bag," said Vlad.

To everyone's surprise, Brenner jerked his head quickly and butted Angelique in the head. It was not Angelique who saw stars but Brenner. "Jeeesus!" he murmured.

"I wish you wouldn't do that again. You'll hurt yourself," said Angelique with a sweet smile.

Brenner seemed dazed, but he managed to ask, "Who are you people?"

"Tell me first, where's Cat?" demanded Vlad.

Brenner chortled. "She's my protection. If you don't want her harmed, you'd better free me."

Chapter 30. In the Nick of Time

I became so frightened by Jack's demeanor that I kicked him in the groin and pushed myself off the table. I crouched in a corner, closed my eyes, and prayed. Suddenly, a loud boom came from the garage. I opened my eyes and saw the office window explode and Mathew come flying through it in a shower of glass shards. He bounced off across the same desk I had occupied just seconds before and hit the wall. He slid down to the floor and collapsed in a lifeless heap.

Jack-Al pulled their guns from their holsters and faced the hole in the window, ready to shoot anything in sight. Instead, the door burst open as if it had no hinges. It hit Al, and Al flew into Jack, and both of them slid off the length of the desk and crashed into the wall, landing on the other side.

I covered my mouth with my fists. What on earth had just happened? Jack-Al were groaning in pain on the floor, one on top of the other.

François stood in the doorway with narrowed eyes and a determined face.

I had never felt more relieved in my life to see someone, and it was none other than François. I ran to him and threw myself into his arms.

He cradled me and asked, "Are you OK? Did they injure you?"

"Thank you, François! You came in the nick of time." I was so glad that he was here with me. "I'm OK. Shaken, but OK." I kept nodding to assure him, and I pulled my skirt down some more.

François noticed that. "Did they touch you?"

"The white brute tried," I said, gesturing with my head in their direction.

Without a word, François moved toward them.

"Careful, they have guns," I said.

He raised his fist and punched down twice. The sound of wood cracking followed each blow. François removed four guns from them, two big ones and two stubby ones, and placed them on the desk. He pulled out his phone and said, "Vlad! Cat is OK."

-VVV-

Vlad turned the phone off and smiled. "Your accomplices, Agent Brenner, are out of commission. And Cat is safe with one of my associates."

Brenner paled. Even in the low light cast by the street lighting he was as white as Vlad or Angelique.

"Since Cat is saved, we will take you someplace where you can tell us everything," said Vlad.

"Wait, wait!" Beads of sweat started forming on Brenner's forehead. "You do realize that our conversation outside in the street was transmitted to my other associates? They'll be looking for me."

"Yes, and you'll tell us who they are," said Vlad. "Besides, all they heard was something about Dracula and his cat."

"Yes, but they know who you are," said Brenner in desperation.

"Do they now? And who am I?"

"You're Dracula. You're a vampire."

"How do you know that?"

"I put two and two together from what your old girl friend told me about you."

"And, Agent Brenner, do you know who these two are?" Vlad pointed to Angelique and Mundibuto.

"Yes, I know who they are. I know everything about you, about your associates, where you live, even that you've been faking conversations in your apartment because you knew you were being tapped. I told you about the tapping."

"Thank you! Good to know that. However, you didn't answer me. Who are these two flanking you?"

"Their names are not important," said Brenner, shaking his head.

"Very well. If I am Dracula the Vampire, wouldn't my associates here, sitting on either side of you, be vampires as well?"

Brenner stared at Vlad to see if he was bluffing. Vlad looked calmly back at him.

Brenner turned his head slowly to his right to check out Angelique. "Holy Mary, mother of God!" Brenner screamed once he took in Angelique the vampire, with bloodshot eyes and fangs thirsty for his blood. Brenner jerked back against Mundibuto. He heard a low growl from his left side. He turned quickly this time and at the sight of Mundibuto he relieved himself and fainted.

Chapter 31. Ghastly

"Did he violate you, Cat?" François asked me again, after he had cracked Jack-Al's skulls.

I shook my head. "But I came pretty close to being gang-raped by those two and who knows, the driver, too." I shuddered.

François picked me up and took me out to the limo. It felt good to be held safe in his arms and sheltered against his firm body.

"Do you want me to take you back to the Red Apartment first, or after I dispose of these thugs?" he asked me.

"Whatever's easier," I said, not understanding what he really intended to do.

"Then, would you mind waiting in the limo's front seat?"

"Sure," I agreed as I recovered my shoes.

Just as I was making myself comfortable in the limo's front passenger seat, I saw François dragging Mathew by the scruff of his neck and dumping him in the trunk of the limo. I doubted he was alive. I heard the rattle of chains back there and François saying something in French. He returned to the office. François threw Al out, and then Jack, through the broken window. He tossed them as if he were tossing rolled carpets. Jack landed on top of Al, which possibly made for a softer landing for Jack, and he stirred.

But not only did he stir, he regained consciousness and stood up. After the way François had hit them – and I heard those cracks – Jack-Al should have been dead. But Jack survived, and he was able to think clearly, because in four steps he was at my door. He yanked it open and pulled me out, grabbing me in a chokehold. François jumped through the window like a tiger ready to kill.

"OK, damn you!" Jack hollered at François. "Get my partner up, or I'll break this bitch's neck." He lifted me off the ground and shook me like a rag doll. I was holding myself on his forearms and trying to wriggle out of his grasp.

François moved quickly toward Al's curled body and with his foot turned Al on his back. He placed his foot on Al's chest. "Maybe he's dead."

"Shake him, damn it!" insisted Jack.

"OK, but I cannot wake the dead." François rocked Al's body with his foot, while staring at Jack.

Al blinked. At first he seemed confused about his situation, but he quickly became lucid. Screaming, he grabbed François's ankle with one hand and his calf with the other. François did not panic; instead, he stepped up on Al's chest, pirouetted on that leg, and when the other leg came down it landed on Al's neck, breaking it. Al went silent and limp. He was surely dead now.

"You mofo!" Jack screamed, and I felt him tighten his forearm on my throat.

But he wasn't quick enough. François grabbed Jack's arms and pried them open. I dropped down from Jack's hold and slithered out from under the two of them. Pushing with my heels, I scurried away. Jack, the big brute, turned red from the effort of resisting the smaller man, although he was a vampire.

François released Jack, squatted, and swiped his leg under the hulk, toppling him. I felt the ground shake. François did not relent. He jumped on the downed man, reached into his crotch and yanked out Jack's genitals. I'd never heard anyone scream in more agony than Jack did while holding his crotch. François held the pink flesh over Jack's head; the dripping blood covered Jack's face.

"That's what you get for touching Cat!" shouted François. As Jack shrieked in pain with his mouth open, François shoved the genitals in Jack's mouth, and he started choking. Quick as a spider, François pulled the belt from Jack's pants and wrapped it around his head and mouth like a gag, pulling on the end of the belt as if pulling at the end of a garrote.

I didn't want to watch, but I was frozen and couldn't move, not even to close my eyes.

Although badly hurt, Jack was a strong man and he still possessed stamina. He rolled over and freed himself from the belt-garrote, spit out his genitals, and jumped to his feet. The front of his khakis was soaked in blood, his face was bloody, and blood dripped from his mouth. Only his protruding, enraged eyes could be seen in his red, blood-soaked face. He cleaned his mouth with the back of his sleeve, held his legs together to stop the bleeding, and pulled a knife out of the other sleeve.

And then I saw what no living person should see.

François the vampire went into a semi-crouched position, mouth open, fangs extending out like daggers, and LED-red eyes seizing his victim. Jack lowered his guard, unsure of what he was seeing, and he mumbled something. It could have been a muffled scream or a prayer. He did not have a chance to do anything else after that because, in a split second, François leaped to Jack's throat and bit his head off.

Jack's head fell on the concrete and bounced like a coconut after it falls from a palm tree. His headless body remained standing, his arms jerking, the knife still in his grasp, as if he were trying to slash François. Blood was squirting out of his severed neck with every beat of his heart.

And then he collapsed, while his convulsing legs thrashed as if he were trying to get up again. The blood pooled quickly around his headless body. After a while, his limbs stopped moving and his body stopped twitching. Jack was out of the fight, out of blood, and out of life.

Chapter 32. Days After

I woke up at midday. My mind was blank, and I felt hungry. As I got out of bed, I realized that this was not my bed in the Fifth Avenue Apartment. It was one of the bedrooms in the Red Apartment. What was I doing here? I was dressed in my cotton nightgown, so I suspected that Angelique had taken care of me again. Did I drink another Long Island Iced Tea? But I did not have a headache or a hangover. So what put me out so soundly? It was time to get up, go to the kitchen, and find something to eat. I was famished and thirsty. My full bottle of water was on my nightstand, and I emptied it without taking a breath.

Outside it was a bright day, and the time on the alarm clock showed 1:17 pm. I must have slept for twelve hours. I tried to think of what I was doing before I got into bed, but I couldn't remember anything other than Jack's thrashing legs. It was strange, remembering the blood, the head bouncing off the concrete floor, the killing of Jack-Al; none of it seemed to bother me that much. I shrugged. I needed to eat something.

The apartment was deserted. I felt like having ham and eggs, so I began cooking in the fully supplied kitchen just for me. Where were Vlad and the others? Where was François? In my mind, I now saw him as the killer vampire. That image did not scare me, either. I made coffee and cooked four eggs, bacon, and hash browns, and toasted four slices of wheat bread.

I wolfed it all down, eating the last slice of bread with strawberry jam. I felt so much better. Where was everyone? I'd better change into something more appropriate for the day. While stretching I wondered, should I go back to my bedroom in the Fifth Avenue Apartment to dress? Something told me to get dressed in this bedroom in the Red Apartment. Surprise, surprise! The closet and dresser had all my clothes, but they were all brand new. Angelique must have shopped for a new set of clothes for me. I didn't remember moving out of my other bedroom on Fifth Avenue. "Be prepared at all times" resonated in my mind. I took a quick shower, put on some makeup, dressed in sweats, and then I ran to the Green Apartment.

They were all there in the big room.

"Hey!" I said and looked at them with some relief. This was my family now. "Sorry, I overslept."

"Good afternoon, Cat!" Vlad said with a big smile.

"Feeling better, hon?" asked Angelique.

"I feel great," I said.

"*Bon jour!*" François greeted me.

"Hey!" Mundibuto said and then addressed the others, "What did I tell you? The stuff always works."

"Stuff? What stuff?" I became suspicious. "What did you give me?"

"Stuff to make you feel better and help you sleep," said Vlad. He rose very slowly and stiffly from his armchair.

"It did help, and now that I've had breakfast, I feel great," I said. "I don't remember ever sleeping so much."

"One and a half days," said Angelique.

"What? What day is today?"

"Friday," said François.

"Friday? How could I have slept for so long?" I looked around at everyone. "What did you give me?" I asked Vlad.

"I gave you something," answered Mundibuto instead. "Strong African medicine. Good for you."

"Good for me!" I yelled. Then I reconsidered. I felt well, rested, and relaxed, and so I asked softly, "What did you give me?"

"African medicine made of many roots and medicinal plants," Mundibuto said as if advertising a miracle potion. "How do you feel?" He looked at me with lowered eyelids, as a concerned doctor might when treating his patient.

"OK, but I want to know why did you give me your African medicine?"

"Because you were a basket case," said Vlad.

"I don't remember that." I tried to recall what had happened one and a half days ago.

"Cat, you were traumatized by what Jack and Al did to you, and then you witnessed their demise," explained Vlad.

Images of Jack on top of me and about to rape me flashed in my mind . . . seeing Al's neck being broken, and then Jack's head being ripped off by François, and then his headless body convulsing on the concrete floor. In spite of these images, I didn't shudder or felt any revulsion.

I looked at Mundibuto. "What else does your medicine do, besides putting me to sleep for so long?"

"In short, it immunizes you from psychological trauma."

"Please elaborate, Mundibuto."

"When someone witnesses a violent death, as you did by seeing a vampire on a murdering spree, it affects their psychological well-being." Mundibuto tapped his temple with a beefy finger. "In many cases, that person may go crazy or become catatonic, and could suffer psychological problems for a lifetime."

"And that medicine cured me?" I asked with appropriate incredulity.

"Yes," said Mundibuto. "Over the ages, the people of Africa have experienced many hardships. Witchdoctors created the stuff I gave you to help people cope and continue a healthy life after their traumatic experiences. It toughens you, it makes you forget, perhaps it makes you callous to bloodshed in a way." He shrugged.

"Callous? To murder?" I asked, but not in the tone of voice I would have used before he gave me the voodoo medication. My God, it worked. It made me less sensitive to the killings I had witnessed and may witness in the future.

"It is true, but necessary, considering what you went through," said Mundibuto.

"Is this something that will last me for the rest of my life?"

"I think so. The long sleep modified your senses," answered Mundibuto.

"Holy shit! I won't be able to be compassionate any more?" I became worried, looking from Mundibuto to Vlad.

"It has nothing to do with being compassionate," said Vlad. "You will be compassionate and have feelings of loss, caring, and empathy, among many others. However, in a way, you will think and experience life like, well, a doctor would."

"A doctor?"

"A doctor, by training, does not suffer from revulsion at the sight of blood. A doctor can amputate someone's leg to save a life, even if that poor soul may be awake and screaming in pain. And afterward the doctor can still enjoy his meal. This is the closest explanation I can give you about how you'll feel from now on when you see blood caused by a crime, torture, or murder."

I should have shuddered and lost my breakfast, but I didn't. "Am I becoming a vampire?"

"No, not at all," Vlad said. He walked to me and gave me a hug. "You are still human."

"Do vampires take this stuff?" I asked Mundibuto.

"No, we don't need to. For vampires, blood is like water. It doesn't bother us a bit."

I suppose I started to think and feel like a vampire then. Would I be able to kill someone from now on and not be bothered in the least? I hoped not. "What did you do with the bodies of my kidnappers?" I asked, more from curiosity than anything else.

"They and the limo are at the bottom of the East River," said François, looking over from his laptop.

"Will they be found?" I asked.

"They might, if they dredge the river or look for them at that specific spot." François didn't seem to be concerned about that possibility. "And the limo will stay at the bottom, weighed down by the heavy chains and shackles loaded in the trunk."

"Are you OK with that, Cat?" asked Vlad.

I nodded, while realizing how cool I was about what they, or François, had done with Jack-Al and the driver. "Veronica set me up," I said, remembering her call.

"We know. You told us when we brought you back," said Angelique.

"And?" I asked.

"She disappeared," Vlad said. "Veronica was an independent operative, working for Brenner. She used Tiffani to get the financial information on you and me. Be careful about Veronica."

"All she wants is money." I shrugged. "Too bad, I'm not finished with her yet." I clenched my teeth and curled my hands into fists.

"Good!" said Vlad, happy to see me so determined.

"François, how did you find me? Wait. I know." I touched my crucifix.

He smiled. "It is still jewelry, but it also has a micro transmitter inside. I gave you the crucifix for your protection. Vlad was worried after Brenner mentioned your name."

"Thank you, Vlad and François."

"All's well that ends well," Vlad said. "Next we have to consider my funeral."

Chapter 33. Time for Action

"Funeral?" I seemed to draw a blank about what he just said.

"My fake death and cremation," said Vlad.

"Oh, yes." I remembered our master plan. "Did you find a suitable body?"

"A perfect match," said Mundibuto with a wide smile.

"The guy in the freezer did not look much like Vlad," I said.

"I took that guy back. The morgue was relieved to find him, finally. They were about to call the police to start an investigation for a body snatcher. And to save someone's job I confessed that I had misplaced the body, for which I was fired on the spot."

"And that's how the career of Mundibuto, the mortician, tragically ends." François sighed.

"It wasn't in you anyway, Mundibuto," giggled Angelique.

"I know, but I'll miss cuddling with those cold and stiff bodies," said a saddened Mundibuto.

"Macabre jokes." I rolled my eyes, although I couldn't help but imagine Mundibuto lying down with a couple of stiffs in one of those locker drawers. "OK, so we have a new body. What do we do and when?"

"It's good that you're up and in good spirits," said Vlad. "We will have my funeral by the time rush hour is underway."

"Today?" I was surprised.

"The man is dead, and he needs to be put to rest before he starts to stink." Mundibuto fanned his nose.

"Where do you have him, in the freezer?" I asked.

"No, upstairs in my bed," said Vlad.

I gasped. "You have a dead man in your bed?" Then I thought, where else?

"I set up your faux voice for you to say good-bye to me earlier this morning, and you departed for a shopping day in the city," said Vlad. "I was asleep, as far as you knew, and did not respond. Angelique impersonated you leaving from the Fifth Avenue entrance. She was followed but gave them the slip downtown. They may still be looking for you there.

"After a tiring day in town, you'll return home soon. To do that, you'll need to wear the same clothes as Angelique wore this morning. Leave by the secret elevator and slip out through the underground garage. Just as a precaution, you'll need to wear a black wig and dark glasses when you exit. Angelique has everything prepared for you. When we give you the signal, toss the wig and the glasses and come back home as yourself."

"Through the Fifth Avenue entrance," I said to make sure.

"Correct," said Vlad. "When you return, act normally and check on me. To your shock, you'll find me dead in my bed. You'll call Dr. Le Bec immediately." Vlad pointed to François. "And then you'll call the paramedics."

"At your service, *mademoiselle*." François bowed. He was dressed in a suit and bowtie. From behind the sofa he lifted a doctor's bag and the head mask of a balding man. That was going to be his disguise.

"Should I act surprised, hysterical, should I cry?"

"All of those," said Vlad. "This is your chance to act as the good great-granddaughter who returns home to find the old man dead, passed away in his sleep."

I gulped. We had talked about and planned this, but now it was show time, real and dangerous. "I hope I'll remember to do all that needs to be done and not screw it up."

"You will do great," said Vlad. "Just in case you have a mental lapse, refer to this." Vlad handed me a bookmark, which had step-by-step instructions and phone numbers to call. "After you get the death certificate, call the mortuary. Everything is as planned and paid for. Then let them do their job."

"What do you want me to do with the ashes?" I asked.

"My fake ashes. Place them on the mantle and then eventually pour them down the drain," said Vlad. "Brenner will have good company down there."

"And don't worry, hon," Angelique said. "I'll be shadowing you, and you'll hear from me every step of the way. Mundibuto will coordinate our transportation, so we can get to the Souls of God Funeral Home and Mortuary quickly. François – I mean, Dr. Le Bec – will be with you when the paramedics arrive, to place the body in the mortuary hearse. You'll swing by the New Age Eastern Church and get one or two of their spiritual monks to accompany you to the mortuary. You'll give them a check for their trouble afterward. Just as we planned." She gave me a wink. "After that, you'll be by yourself, as Vlad did not have any friends and you are his only family."

"Ready, Cat?" asked Vlad.

"Let's get it over with."

Chapter 34. Dealer Is Dead

"Field Agent Pratt reporting from Dealer's location." The instant message appeared on Johnson's screen. "Joker has returned home." Johnson sighed with relief. He and the rest of the team looked like fumbling morons. Special Agent Miller was missing and had not surfaced yet. No one knew his whereabouts. Pratt lost Joker this morning, and now she's waltzing back home without anyone knowing what she did all day. "I'm glad she found you, Pratt," Johnson messaged back.

Pratt did not respond.

Smith came into the office. "Any news on our lost Joker?"

"Yeah, she just returned home," said Johnson. "They're both home now, although I didn't hear all day from Dealer. What are the chances that he, too, gave us the slip?"

Smith did not comment on that. "They found Miller's car."

"What? Where?"

"On 40th, in an underground garage," answered Smith. "CIS is working on the –"

"Shhh," interrupted Johnson. "She's in the apartment." He increased the volume on the speaker icon, and both of them listened.

"Hey, Vlad!" Joker called out. "I'm so tired! My feet hurt, and I didn't find a thing to buy."

"It's terrible to be rich and not be able to buy a thing," Johnson commented sarcastically, shaking his head.

"How was your day?" asked Joker. Her footsteps could be heard in the kitchen. "Vlad? Are you asleep?"

Johnson and Smith listened as Joker walked through the apartment.

"You're not in your office," she said as she walked farther down the hallway. She knocked softly at a door, presumably his bedroom, and opened it. "Vlad?" she asked from inside his bedroom. "Vlad, are you OK? Vlad? Vlad! Oh, my God!" she screamed at the top of her lungs.

Smith and Johnson jumped to their feet. Something was wrong.

"She's calling someone," said Johnson.

"Hello, this is Dr. Le Bec," a man answered.

"Dr. Le Bec, this is Cat Sanders, Vlad Draculesti's great-granddaughter. Please come quickly. Vlad is not moving. He doesn't look good. I need help, please. Oh my God, oh my God, oh my God!"

"Please stay calm, Cat. Is he breathing? Can he talk? Are his eyes open?"

"No, no. He's not moving at all. He's in his bed."

"I'll come over immediately, and please call 911."

"Who's this Dr. Le Bec?" Johnson wondered aloud, as he clicked on a few search keys. "And she's calling 911."

"I think something happened to Dealer," said Smith. "Should we send Pratt inside?"

"On what grounds?" Johnson objected. "Let the paramedics help out, and we'll listen to what's going on."

"Where is goddamn Miller?" exploded Smith.

"Shhh. I think she's crying now," said Johnson with a neighborly curiosity.

"Did headquarters tell us any other news about Miller's whereabouts?" asked Smith.

"No, but the FBI is on it."

"Some good they did. The NYPD found his car."

"She's still crying. I think Dealer's kicked the bucket." Johnson's eyes widened.

"What are we supposed to do now?"

Johnson shrugged. "We're assigned to monitor them. It seems there is a medical emergency over there, so let's see how it develops."

Johnson texted Field Agent Pratt to stand by, and then asked Smith, "Any sign of foul play?"

"About whom are you asking?"

"Miller! He's been missing for almost two days," said Johnson.

"No, but there is something I heard about him," said Smith in confidence.

Johnson looked up.

"Miller might be an alcoholic. You know, one of those weekend alcoholics who fall into a bottle and it takes them several days to come out of it."

"You think he's in some cheap hotel room right now, drying out?" speculated Johnson.

"Or still filling up," said Smith.

Johnson pointed to the screen, and both agents read the instant message from Pratt: "FDNY EMS are here. Something's really going on."

"Dealer may be dead," messaged Johnson back. "Stand by."

A minute later they heard the paramedics entering the apartment and Joker taking them immediately to Dealer's bedroom.

The paramedic team exchanged information, made terse comments, and then one said, "No need to take his vitals. Rigor mortis has set in. He's gone."

Johnson's eyes widened some more. "What the fuck?"

"From what I'm hearing, Dealer is dead, for real." With a smirk on his face, Smith shook his head.

The downstairs doorman called in, announcing Dr. Le Bec, and, a minute later, he entered the apartment and engaged the paramedics in conversation.

"I'm Dr. Le Bec. Mr. Draculesti is my patient. What are his vitals?"

"Dr. Le Bec, I'm Chuck Farmer, EMT lead. Your patient is deceased. My estimation is that he died eight to ten hours ago. Did he suffer from any medical conditions?"

"Yes, I treated him for cardiovascular disease," said Dr. Le Bec. "I prescribed medication for ischemic cardiomyopathy." Le Bec made indistinct noises, probably checking the patient.

"Unfortunately, he most probably died of a massive heart attack."

"Yes, we took an inventory of the medication on his night stand, and we came to the same conclusion," said the paramedic.

More muffled noises could be heard as Dr. Le Bec continued examining the deceased. "I'm sorry, Cat. He's gone."

Joker began crying and wailing.

Chuck Farmer stepped in. "I'm sorry for your loss, Ms. Draculesti. I'd like to ask you a few questions, if I may."

"No, my name is Sanders, Catherina Sanders," Cat said between sobs. "Mr. Draculesti is my great-grandfather."

"When was the last time you saw Mr. Draculesti alive?"

"Last night." Cat began crying again.

"How about this morning?"

"I said good-bye to him when I left the apartment this morning, When I returned a half-hour ago and didn't see him walking around, I came into his bedroom and I found him." Cat's voice was raspy from crying.

"Did you know about his condition?"

"Yes. He wrote Dr. Le Bec's phone number on the white board in the kitchen. And I had his number on my speed dial."

"Again, I'm sorry about your loss," said the paramedic. "Dr. Le Bec, as his physician, would you sign the death certificate?"

"Yes, I will, and there is no need to take him to the medical examiner. You're already overworked with other important cases."

"Yes, thank you for your understanding," said Farmer. "Miss, did you make funeral arrangements for him?"

"Yes, we had. Everything is arranged."

Johnson and Smith looked at each other dumbfounded.

"Un-fucking-believable. He's dead," said Johnson.

"So much for the undead, the living-forever bullshit," Smith said, breaking the clean language protocol, which Johnson always ignored.

"Someone will have to do some explaining about reopening this bullshit case," said Johnson, shaking his head.

The two agents continued listening to the ongoing commotion as the paramedics departed and Joker called the New Age Eastern Church and asked for a holy escort and funeral preparations.

"Do you get the sense that this whole affair is happening rather fast?" wondered Smith.

"I see nothing wrong with what she's doing," said Johnson. "She called that hocus-pocus church for a holy man, and she probably made mortuary arrangements well before we came snooping around. She's getting ready for his funeral."

"That church, the New Age Eastern Church – didn't Dealer convert to that religion not that long ago?" Smith inquired on his computer about the church and opened up the church's website. He began reading about the New Age Eastern religion, while Johnson looked over his shoulder.

"What are you looking for?" Johnson asked.

After reading some more, Agent Smith pointed to the screen and said, "This religion says that the devotee must be cremated within six hours after the death is discovered in order for the soul to be picked up by the Eternal Ship from Heaven."

"So?" Agent Johnson scratched his head. "The Jews and the Muslims bury their dead within a day."

"So that's why she's in such a hurry," said Smith, pondering. "In that case, his body will be ashes in the next five hours."

Chapter 35. Heavenly Bodies Transference

The instant messaging beeped. "Agent Pratt reporting: A black hearse has pulled up in front of Dealer's domicile." Johnson stared at Smith.

Smith pulled his cell phone out. "Pratt, what is the name of the mortuary on that hearse?"

"Heavenly Bodies Transference, sir," replied Agent Pratt.

Smith typed the name into his computer and found a website. He read aloud the marketing spiel: "We transport fast and for less all defunct bodies from home to the coroner, to the mortuary, between mortuaries, to cemeteries, by ground or air."

"Fast service for less," quipped Johnson. "No delays in meeting the eternal motherfucking ship."

Smith searched for the New Age Church on his computer again. "They're located in midtown."

"Yeah, and?" wondered Johnson.

"They'll stop to pick up their holy man," said Smith. "We need to pick up their trail at that location."

"Field Agent Pratt is already in position to follow them," said Johnson.

"I don't like this." Smith suspected something. "Joker is moving too fast to get rid of the body. We'd better reinforce Pratt."

"Hmm," considered Johnson. "Listen – the good Dr. Le Bec is leaving Joker by herself." He pointed to the speaker.

"What do you expect? He's a doctor, not a mortician," said Smith.

"Somehow, he sounded rather friendly with Joker," said Johnson. "I expected him to be with her, and –"

"And what? Get lucky?" said Smith sarcastically. "Let's go, we're wasting daylight hours."

Johnson frowned but followed Smith.

Smith and Johnson exited their secret underground garage in a nondescript sedan. Smith was at the wheel.

"Pratt, this is Smith. We're heading for the New Age Eastern Church where we believe the hearse will be heading. Please keep this communication channel open."

"Yes, sir," came the reply. "Anything I should be aware of?"

"Nothing specific. I am suspicious about Joker's intentions. Let's not lose sight of her."

"Understood. Wait. They're loading the body in the hearse."

"Good – keep an eye on the situation."

"Joker did not get in the hearse. She's going back into the building. Should I follow the hearse?"

Agents Smith and Johnson exchanged irritated looks. Only one field agent in place, a hearse moving away with the deceased Dealer, and Joker may stay home or take another ride to the mortuary.

"The dead are less important than the living. Stay with Joker," Smith told Pratt.

"How about the hearse?" Johnson asked.

"We'll intersect the hearse on Fifth Avenue. They're coming our way." Smith pressed on the gas and headed toward Fifth.

"I'll contact the NYPD traffic controller." Johnson pulled out the keyboard on his smart phone and entered several codes in it. "This is Agent Johnson," he said into his Bluetooth mic. "We are looking for a hearse heading down Fifth Avenue . . . What color? Black, and the name of the company on the door is Heavenly Bodies Transference . . . You spotted it? Where is it heading?" Johnson turned to Smith. "They say that it just turned on 59th Street."

"They're taking the Queensboro Bridge," said Smith.

"Any other similar vehicle in the vicinity of Fifth?" Johnson asked the dispatcher, and, after a moment of listening, he said, "Please track this vehicle of interest and report every minute. Thanks!"

"I guess they're not in that much of a hurry after all," quipped Smith.

"They're paid by the hour," said Johnson. "Maybe they're going to a mortuary in Queens."

"Joker just boarded a limo," announced Field Agent Pratt on the radio.

"Stay with Joker," said Smith. "She'll be going to the New Age Eastern Church on 35th, between Seventh and Eighth Avenues. We're following the hearse over the Queensboro Bridge."

"They're heading out of Manhattan," smirked Johnson. "Manhattan funeral homes are too expensive for Joker."

"They're on Queens Boulevard," said Johnson. "We're in Queens."

"Pratt, where is Joker heading?" asked Smith.

"Down Fifth, and now they're turning on 35th," replied Pratt.

"This damn traffic," shouted Smith. "Pratt, where are you now?"

"In front of the New Age Eastern Church. Two men in pink robes just entered the limo, joining Joker."

"Good. Keep after her. She must be going where the body will be," said Smith.

"This is Agent Pratt. Joker and the monks are heading down Broadway."

"They're planning to take the Brooklyn Bridge?" Johnson wondered.

"Keep after them, Pratt." Smith addressed Johnson: "I wonder how these arrangements were made without us knowing a thing."

"You mean the funeral?"

"Yes, and we still don't know where they'll be taking the body."

"They could have made the arrangements long ago," said Johnson. "They are called pre-need."

"Maybe," but Smith sounded doubtful.

Johnson accessed his smart phone and entered another request. "I asked to check with Heavenly Bodies Transference and find out where that hearse is going. And the NYPD dispatcher confirms that the hearse is heading down Queens Boulevard."

"This is Agent Pratt. Joker and the monks did not take the Brooklyn Bridge. Instead, they took the FDR south."

Smith and Johnson did a quick take.

"Joker and the monks are flying to JFK," said Johnson, and he entered more commands on his smart phone.

"Pratt, I think they're heading for the heliport," said Smith.

"Bingo!" Johnson was reading on his smart phone. "There is a helicopter reserved for JFK."

"We'll meet them at JFK," said Smith with a satisfied smile.

"Better news," said Johnson. "Heavenly Bodies Transference has a hearse scheduled for JFK. That must be our hearse. Wait, they have another hearse en route going to the heliport." Johnson raised his eyebrows.

"This is Agent Pratt. Joker and the monks are boarding a helicopter."

"What is the tail number?" asked Smith.

As Agent Pratt spelled out the series of letters and numbers, Johnson entered them onto the phone's expanded keyboard. "This one is not flying to JFK but somewhere in Brooklyn, and the reservation was made in Cat Sanders's name."

"This is Agent Pratt. There is a white hearse that was parked right behind the helicopter, which just took off."

Smith almost rear-ended the car in front of them as he exchanged bewildered looks with Johnson.

Johnson checked the information on his smart phone and turned red. "I'll be. The white hearse was scheduled to pick up a body from Dealer's address and deliver it to the heliport, and the black one was scheduled for a pick-up at JFK."

"Shit!" screamed Smith. "What did the black hearse pick up at Dealer's address?"

"Pratt," said Johnson. "Did you see a body being loaded onto the black hearse, back on Fifth?"

"Positive. I saw a gurney with a body bag on it, and it was loaded onto the black hearse," answered Pratt.

Johnson entered more text on his phone. "Son of a bitch!" he shouted after he read the reply. "What the black hearse picked up in front of Dealer's apartment was a bag with funeral clothes for the stiff they would be picking up from JFK." Johnson sighed and wiped his face with his hand.

"And the helicopter that just took off?" Smith asked.

"The helicopter must have Dealer's body, along with Joker and the monks, and it is scheduled to land at Dyker Beach Park in Brooklyn." Johnson read another message on his phone. "The white hearse must have arrived after Joker left in her limo, which Pratt followed."

"Fucking unbelievable how they fooled us!" shouted Smith. He made an illegal U-turn on Queens Boulevard the first chance he got, raising a blare of car horns and traffic chaos.

"Are we authorized to take a helicopter?" Johnson asked.

"I don't know. Miller had that information," said Smith.

"Agent Pratt, see if you can take a helicopter and follow Joker," said Johnson.

"Am I authorized to spend that kind of money?" Pratt asked.

"Just do it, Pratt." Smith was fuming.

"Are you authorizing this expense, Agent Smith?"

Smith checked his rearview mirror. "Goddamn it!" He hit the steering wheel. "Fuck, the cops are after us." With lights flashing, the police were about to pull them over.

Chapter 36. The Funeral

"Cat, we're almost there," Angelique said into my ear bud. "That yummy agent who followed you is at a loss over your departure by helicopter."

The helicopter took off. I could see the agent on the ground with his hands on his hips, talking agitatedly into his Bluetooth. I was exhausted from the whole ordeal: First, finding a dead man who looked like Vlad in his bed, then crying – and I was sincerely crying, seeing that person so pale and so dead – calling François, who impersonated Dr. Le Bec, and trembling with fear when the paramedics arrived. These people were professionals and doing their jobs, and we had no control over them. What if they had discovered our sham? They could have taken the body to the coroner, although Mundibuto assured me that if this had happened he would have stolen the body from the morgue.

But it worked. The paramedics were more than happy not to have to take the body with them; Dr. Le Bec was very convincing, and we got the death certificate. I wondered what was happening at the other end, to the people who were listening to us. Would they have stormed the apartment to make sure Vlad was indeed dead? Luckily, they didn't do that.

With my binoculars, I saw the agent outside not follow the black hearse, which was loaded with a body bag full of clothes. Then we delayed the white hearse that came for the dead body until after I had left by limo to pick up the divine escorts. I was relieved when I saw the agent following me to the New Age Eastern Church. Unless they had another agent keeping watch, the white hearse would arrive at the Fifth Avenue Apartment, and François – Dr. Le Bec – would load the body to be taken to the heliport.

As far as I knew, no one had tailed the white hearse with the body, and, by the time we arrived at the heliport with the two holy escorts, the body was already loaded into the helicopter. And here we were, flying to Dyker Beach Park in Brooklyn.

It took only a few minutes to arrive at the park, and, as soon as we landed, the Souls of God Funeral Home and Mortuary hearse whisked the body to the funeral home. A limo was waiting for us, and the driver was Mundibuto, with dark glasses, a driver's cap, and all.

At the Souls of God Funeral Home and Mortuary, we found the body placed in an ornate and very expensive casket, for which I'm sure the mortuary owners were more than appreciative of the money they made from that sale. Beautiful crowns of white flowers adorned the casket and the sides of the room. There was no embalming, and, according to Vlad's new-found religion, the faster the flames consumed his body, the sooner his ascent to heaven.

Soft organ music and an angelic choir sounded in the background. The holy escorts performed their ceremony and prepared Vlad's fake body and soul for the eternal journey. It was beautiful, and I cried again. I knew that Vlad would not have such a ceremony, and it was good that we had this one in his name.

After the short-but-sweet ceremony ended, the two divine escorts and I followed the casket down the hall to the crematorium. I had never seen a crematorium before, so I didn't know what to expect. It looked like a boiler room, and it smelled unpleasantly like dust, ashes, and stuff I couldn't identify. The crematorium attendant opened the iron door and pulled a blackened, hefty metal tray out, and he rolled the casket from the gurney onto the tray. He then pushed the casket inside.

The door closed with a clang, and I jumped a little, thinking of the finality of that sound and of the body's existence here on Earth. The mortuary attendant gave us a final moment to pray. I ignored the holy escorts and the prayers they were chanting, and I prayed my rosary. I presumed the dead man was a Christian and deserved a Christian prayer. Once we had finished, the attendant pushed a big green button. A whooshing sound accompanied the ignition, and fire engulfed the casket. I sat and waited for a few minutes, and then left the cremation room.

I requested a cab to take the holy escorts back to Manhattan, and I gave them a check for their kind farewell for my dearly departed. It took three hours to receive the urn with the ashes. The urn was made of bronze, and it was still warm when they handed it to me. Actually, it was on a dolly, and when I tried to lift it I found I couldn't. Mundibuto picked it up and took it to the limo, and that was it. It's sad how you can exist one minute, and the next you're dust.

"Miss Catherina Sanders, may we have a word with you?" I heard someone calling my name, as I was about to get into the limo. A heavyset Latino man, dressed in a dark grey suit, approached me. He removed his wallet, opened it, and showed me his ID. It had his picture, name, a number and the US Department of Homeland Security's blue seal with an eagle. "I am Agent Johnson with Homeland Security."

A second massively built, similarly dressed blonde man opened his ID wallet. "I am Agent Smith with Homeland Security."

Luckily, I had large dark glasses on so they didn't see me blink. They had managed to catch up with me. "Homeland Security? What is this all about?"

"Ma'am, we would like to see the death certificate for Mr. Vlad Draculesti," said Agent Smith. Both Smith and Johnson, their ties askew, were drenched in sweat, as if they had run for miles.

"Do you mean my great-grandfather?" I opened the door and showed them the urn, which was strapped in the back seat. "He passed away from a massive heart attack. I'm sure his death certificate is in a public file, and you can review it at your convenience." I was not about to show them the certificate, although the funeral home had a copy just inside.

Agent Smith chewed on his lip, unsure of what to say.

"Ma'am, why did you cremate your great-grandfather's body so expeditiously?" Agent Smith asked.

"Religious considerations, if you must know. Not everyone wishes to have his body injected with chemicals and then buried six feet under. May I ask you, what is your concern about this?"

"This is a Homeland Security matter, ma'am," said Agent Johnson.

"My great-grandfather's funeral is a Homeland Security matter? Don't you have better things to do, like catching some terrorists? My great-grandfather was surely not a terrorist. I'm appalled by your insinuations. If you want to discuss this matter any further, contact my lawyers."

"We will do that, ma'am," said Agent Smith. "And rest assured that you are a person of interest to us as well."

"If you are implying that I did something criminal to my great-grandfather, that would be an NYPD problem, not yours. Good day!" I got into the limo and shut the door behind me. Mundibuto drove away, leaving the two agents standing in the parking lot, unsure of what to do next. I turned around to see them enter the mortuary.

"I think you handled that very well," said Mundibuto through the opened glass partition.

"That was odd," I said. "It was as if they were grasping at straws."

"I think they are very confused about this turn of events," said Angelique into my ear bud.

"Let's go home," said Mundibuto.

"Vlad, can you hear me?" I asked.

"Yes, Cat. I can hear you loud and clear, and you did a super job. I almost cried myself."

"Thanks! Do you have a lawyer, in case I need one for this pestilence?"

"Of course we do, or you do now. First, Yakowitz will handle the financial matters since you've just inherited all I had. And as far as these Homeland Security agents are concerned, I have several lawyers, should the need arise. We'll talk more when you get home."

I sank down into the seat and into my thoughts about this entire situation. Without a doubt, I was a criminal now. I hadn't killed anyone, but I had faked the death of Vlad Draculesti, who was still alive.

When I arrived home, I asked the doorman to help me with the urn. The man offered me his condolences and helped me with the bronze container. I placed it on the mantle in a place of honor. I took a shower and cleansed myself of the sorrow I had experienced. I was concerned about not knowing what would happen next, not for me so much, but for Vlad.

Should I turn on my fake voice? I was alone, and I don't normally talk to myself. Instead, I turned on the radio to the classical music station WWFM and listened for a while before going over to the Red Apartment. There, everyone was in the great room with big smiles on their faces. Vlad was lying in an easy chair.

François popped the cork on a bottle of Dom Perignon and offered me the first glass. After he'd filled everyone's glass, he said, "Here's to Cat: the natural-born actress and con artist."

"Hear, hear!" they saluted.

I took a long sip and I felt better. "Well, I think we did pretty well. And I'm sorry, Vlad, to have your fake ashes on the mantle."

"You did great, Cat," said Vlad.

"Are you sure you're dying?"

"I don't have much longer, Cat," said Vlad sadly. "However, that's life. We all have to go one day."

I saw Angelique wiping an eye. Mundibuto interlaced his fingers behind his shaved head as if to release tension. François refilled my glass.

"I have to admit that I'm very proud of you, Cat," said Vlad. "You are the brains who concocted this deceptive plan."

I thought, it's true: I had the idea of the double body. I am a master criminal. My parents would not appreciate this dark fact about their daughter, if they were still alive.

"And you managed this very well. Very well. You're a natural carnivore," Vlad concluded.

"What do you mean, I'm a natural carnivore?"

Mundibuto laughed. "Cat, in this world, there are carnivores, scavengers, parasites, and herbivores. You are a carnivore."

I was stunned at what he said, and my face must have shown it.

"Hon, that's a compliment," said Angelique. "Although you are a noble carnivore."

"Oh, yeah," agreed François.

"Carnivores eat the herbivores," I said. "It sounds like the exploiters and the exploited."

"You could interpret it that way, however, it has a different meaning," said Vlad. "The natural world is made of fighters and flighters. Most herbivores are flighters, and most carnivores are fighters. And then you have the scavengers who sit on the fence and come down when death rules. The parasites will suck the blood of carnivores, scavengers, and herbivores alike. Therefore, you are a fighter, a carnivore."

"I gather I was living a very quiet and sheltered life until now," I said.

"So you thought," said Vlad. "Sooner or later, your true spirit would have risen."

"Now I know that I can take care of myself, unless I have a brute on top of me trying to rape me." I trembled.

"Even then, did you lie down without a fight?" Vlad asked.

I thought for a moment and then I shook my head. They were right – I was a fighter.

"Are you at ease with who you are?" Angelique asked.

I nodded and then remembered that it wasn't over yet. "What are we going to do about Homeland Security?"

"Nothing. They're at a loss," said Vlad. "I was their principal person of interest, and I am ashes now. You are left, Cat, and you're not a vampire."

"What if they continue their investigation?"

"On what grounds?" Vlad asked. "You came home and found me dead. The paramedics and a doctor were present. Two religious men and the mortuary staff were present at my funeral and cremation." Vlad shrugged.

"There are loose ends," I said. "Four people are dead."

"Three criminals are fish food," said François calmly. "No one knows their whereabouts."

"There are records showing that the limo picked me up that night," I said.

"No such records exist at the limo company," said Mundibuto. "Al and Jack were in the process of committing a crime. They did not leave any record of picking you up. The limo is missing from the fleet, but that's all."

"And Brenner, the dirty agent, is missing," said Vlad.

"How about Dr. Le Bec and the double hearses?" I persisted.

"If they check for Dr. Le Bec, they'll find that he's returned to Canada," said François.

"As for the other hearse, which was another of your brilliant ideas," said Vlad, "someone, who cannot be connected with you or me – even postmortem – ordered a hearse for the Fifth Avenue address. The first body bag was unloaded from a van that obscured the watching agent's view. He saw the loading of a body bag, and presumed it came from my apartment. The doorman downstairs saw my body being taken out through the entrance doors and loaded into a white hearse."

"In spite of that, we should be prepared for the investigation," I said. "Vlad, you may not want to go back to the Fifth Avenue Apartment."

"I agree with you," said Vlad. "I've moved in here, and, if I need something, you can bring it to me. I brought Elena's painting into my new bedroom."

"And we cleaned up any remains of the body you found in Vlad's bedroom," Angelique said.

Vlad looked happy, although he was dying. "For what it is worth, may God have mercy on Tom Brenner's soul."

"That was not Tom Brenner, that was Jack Miller!" I stood up, worried.

Chapter 37. The Aftermath

"That was Tom Brenner," said Vlad. "We nabbed him on the night you were kidnapped. He used the alias John Miller, a special agent working for Homeland Security."

"At Rockefeller Center, Veronica introduced him as her dad," I said. "She did not want to elaborate on why her surname was not Miller. Now I see that she couldn't be a Miller."

"Did you recognize him as John Miller when he was dead in Vlad's bed?" Angelique asked.

"Yes," I said.

"I did my magic makeup on him and made him look as much like Vlad as possible," said Angelique. "No need for the fake passport to identify the deceased." Angelique burst into laughter.

"Why are you laughing?" I asked.

"Because you were shedding real tears when you saw the corpse," she said. "I thought you were acting."

"Maybe. Partly. But also because he looked so much like Vlad. I could see how Vlad would look dead." Tears rolled down my cheeks.

Angelique embraced me. "That's all right, hon."

"Then, no sad feelings for him?" asked Vlad.

I shook my head and wiped my face. "Did he suffer?"

"No, he didn't even wake up from what I gave him," said Mundibuto. "He died in his sleep of a heart attack."

François opened another bottle of Dom Perignon, and he filled my glass. I downed it in one gulp. That was not good; the bubbly almost came back up through my nose.

"For sure, they'll have a big investigation about his disappearance. He was a federal agent," I said, after recovering from my effervescent experience.

"Yes, there will be an investigation," Vlad said. "Remember, he had nothing to do with you, and you'll not be a suspect. However, he was wired, and the conversation between him and me was recorded by no one other than Veronica. Brenner told us everything. The best part is that he addressed me as Dracula."

"We must find Veronica Seyler and Tiffani Arlin," I said.

"Tiffani Arlin quit her job the day you and François encountered her at Rockefeller Center. She suspected she would be fired," said Vlad. "Veronica was fired the following day, the day of the kidnapping. Could Veronica and Tiffani have worked together with Brenner?"

"I don't think so." I was pretty sure. "I think they work for two different entities, and I suspect that Vlad is what attracted them to Yakowitz's employment."

Vlad thought for a moment. "We know that Brenner was after me, and we could say with certainty that Veronica worked with or for him – as a federal agent or a crook, we'll have to find out. As for Tiffani, the only other interested party in me would be Hellinherr."

"François, you may be in danger, too," I was getting worried.

"From now on I'll have a special interest in Tiffani," said François. "I pray to God that she's not involved with Hellinherr."

"First things first," said Vlad. "We need to know Veronica Seyler's real identity and interest in this."

We all nodded in agreement. Homeland Security and the US government were a bigger danger than Hellinherr, if Veronica was a federal agent.

"What shall I do with Brenner's ashes?" I asked.

"As I said, dump him down the drain." Vlad said dismissively. "He'll be at home in the sewer."

Down the sewer? Sad. "Does he have children, a family?"

"No," said Vlad. "He was a drunk. Divorced three times and no kids."

I nodded. It seemed that we had covered all our tracks, except for Veronica and Tiffany, and there was not much remorse for the dearly departed. "What do we do from now on?" I asked.

"Hopefully they'll give up investigating me," said Vlad. "I will stay in this apartment until I die."

I exhaled. If what I had experienced so far was painful, the worst was yet to come. "Are you hurting?"

"No, I have absolutely no pain," said Vlad. "I will not experience any as I deteriorate. However, I'll become weaker. As a matter of fact, despite it being night, I need to sleep already. I will be sleeping more and more." He got up slowly and went to his bedroom.

Seeing him go, I was about to cry.

Angelique put her arm around me. "Would you like to stay with us down here?"

"I would, but I'd better keep up appearances and sleep in my own bed." I wished them good night and retired to the Fifth Avenue Apartment.

Chapter 38. The Master Criminal Mind

In his office at the Department of Homeland Security in Virginia, Assistant Deputy Director Randy Jaworski's round pink face turned beet-red in color. His jaw muscles were flexing as he read the e-report from Johnson and Smith. He lifted his eyes from the tablet and glared at agents Johnson and Smith, who sat nervously across from his desk.

"In my entire career, I've never heard of a more fucked-up surveillance than this one," he finally said. "You have nothing to show about Vlad Draculesti – no friends, no important associates other than lawyers, no terrorist connections, and no suspicious activities. The only family is this Catherina Sanders, who magically appeared in his life at the 24-hour café before the video of them was taken. The suspect died, under your very noses, and Catherina Sanders cremates him within three hours after she discovers his body, while the three of you go on a wild goose chase after them. What do you have to say about that?"

Agents Johnson and Smith looked at each other, not sure of what to say or who should answer him.

Agent Smith inhaled. "Well, sir, the person of interest . . . I mean, his death came as a surprise to us. We were only monitoring him. The paramedics and Draculesti's doctor arrived at the scene, after his great-granddaughter found him dead. Agent

Miller is missing, and we still don't know where he is, and we had limited guidelines about what to do."

"Hmm." The assistant deputy director sighed. "I'll have to get some more facts from you. Did you find any family relationship between Draculesti and Sanders?"

"No, nor did she ever exist in his life before the café incident," said Agent Johnson, finding the courage to speak. "The doorman said that he saw her for the first time with Draculesti the evening following the pushing incident. Soon after that, Draculesti informed the building's staff that she was his great-granddaughter."

"Did you know he had a medical condition?"

"No, nothing from our eavesdropping," said Agent Johnson. "It never occurred to us, considering his alleged life span."

"We had no indication from the ongoing conversations that he suffered from a heart condition," added Agent Smith.

"What information did you obtain from the paramedics, his doctor, and the mortuary staff?" asked Jaworski.

"The paramedics said there was nothing suspicious about his death, and they identified Vlad Draculesti when we showed them his picture. The mortuary staff identified the deceased as well."

Agent Smith swallowed hard. "Dr. Le Bec is a different situation. He is a private practitioner from Canada with a license to practice in New York State."

"And he's disappeared. Just like Agent Miller," Jaworski said. "Are you satisfied with this turn of events?"

Agents Smith and Johnson shook their heads.

"How about this Veronica Seyler who was spotted with Agent Miller?"

"She worked for Abe Yakowitz's law office, and she was fired. She is nowhere to be found," said Agent Smith. "We didn't know about her and Agent Miller until we were forwarded pictures of the two of them from your office. We checked her residence, but she's gone."

"Did you identify her in our database?"

"We couldn't, because the pictures we have of her are with sunglasses on," said Agent Johnson.

"And Tiffani Arlin?"

"Same thing with her, sir," said Agent Smith. "We checked with Yakowitz's office, and she never returned to work the day after the Rockefeller Plaza incident. She and Veronica Seyler vanished."

"How about this François Le Beau, who was photographed by our agent at Rockefeller Plaza at the same time as Sanders, Agent Miller, Seyler, and Arlin?" asked Jaworski.

"We don't have any knowledge of him or his whereabouts," replied Agent Johnson. "He wore dark glasses as well, and we couldn't get the face recognition software to identify him. Just like Seyler and Arlin. There are four people in this investigation who don't seem to have an identity in any domestic database."

Johnson and Smith exchanged glances and shook their heads, supporting each other in their dismay over the disappearances.

"Let me sum it up for you," said Assistant Deputy Director Jaworski, looking stoic. "Agent Miller knew Veronica Seyler, and we cannot find them. Tiffany Arlin was in a lover's quarrel with François Le Beau, and we cannot find them. Dr. Le Bec is missing. Vlad Draculesti, who was our person of interest, is dead and cremated. The only person who knew all these people and is still around is Catherina Sanders." Randy Jaworski raised his eyebrows. "And Catherina Sanders inherited Vlad Draculesti's estate."

Agents Johnson and Smith stared at each other, not quite sure of what to make of that statement.

"Sir." Agent Smith cleared his throat. "Are you implying that while we were observing Vlad

Draculesti, Cat Sanders murdered him for his money?"

"What do you think?"

"And she did all this with the help of Veronica Seyler, Tiffani Arlin, François Le Beau, Dr. Le Bec, and Agent John Miller?" asked Smith incredulously.

"All of them or some of them. And the ones who were not part of the plot, shall we say, could be fish food by now."

"Sir, this means that Cat Sanders is one of the biggest master criminal minds in the world," said Agent Smith.

"Sir," interjected Agent Johnson. "We checked her out. She's a nobody."

"That nobody may be long dead, and the Cat Sanders you dealt with is a hardened criminal who took her place," said Jaworski. "I suggest you two interrogate her and keep monitoring her."

"But, sir," objected Agent Smith. "Shouldn't the FBI be involved in this?"

"They are investigating the disappearances of the missing persons separately from our investigation. You, in the meanwhile, don't let Cat Sanders out of your sight."

"Yes, sir!" Agents Smith and Johnson said as they stood up.

"And one more thing. I've assigned Special Agent Jane Kelly to take charge of this investigation. She will meet you at the New York office tomorrow."

Dismissed, Agents Smith and Johnson left Assistant Deputy Director Jaworski's office with their butts chewed but relieved that they didn't get written reprimands.

Jaworski leaned back in his chair and waited. The sliding doors from his private conference room opened, and an Army major general came in.

He sat in the seat Smith had warmed earlier and said, "Why are you sending them on a wild goose chase?"

"Not at all, General Gonzalez," said Assistant Deputy Director Jaworski. "She is our only link to Vlad Draculesti. He pulled off his own fake death, and she helped him. She knows his whereabouts, and, when she contacts him, we'll take him into custody. Unfortunately, your men identified the dark energy field on the video too late. We could have arrested him before he faked his own death and disappeared."

"Do you think he's out of the country?"

"He knew we were after him. He's probably in Transylvania by now."

Chapter 39. The Blue Sapphire

"How do you feel, Vlad?" I asked.

He smiled. "Better when I see you, Cat."

"You're not drinking your alcohol fuel. Did you lose your appetite?"

"I'm not converting the alcohol into energy anymore. That part of my body has shut down." Vlad moved his hand, slowly pointing to his stomach.

"Are you going to die of starvation?"

"Long before starvation, I'll die from my muscles ceasing to function. Not many days now left."

I didn't know what to say. He was dying for sure, and his deterioration was accelerating. He had not only become whiter but his skin was now translucent. I was able to see some of the muscles, and most of his blue arteries and veins. His lips were dark purple, rather than the pink they used to be. He looked more and more like a corpse. "How do you know the symptoms?"

Vlad took a deep breath, which he was taking more often since his condition worsened. "I read a very old papyrus, which described the death of a high priest in Egypt. I am sure he was a vampire, and he died as well. He had the same symptoms I'm experiencing now."

I lowered my head.

"How are you doing?" he asked.

"As well as circumstances permit." I buried my face in my hands.

"Where is Angelique?"

"She's pretending to be me, in the Fifth Avenue Apartment."

"Good, good. You need to maintain appearances. We're not out of the woods yet. Did you contact the lawyers?"

"Yes. I'm going out to have lunch with them soon to get acquainted with them. They'll return with me shortly before two o'clock to assist me with the so-called meeting with the Homeland Security agents."

"Which of the agents?"

"They have a new special agent, Jane Kelly, who took over from John Miller. She told me that. Agents Smith and Johnson will be there, too."

"Be careful," said Vlad.

"I will. My only worries are Veronica Seyler and Tiffani Arlin. Why did they flee? Mundibuto and François couldn't locate them. Veronica used the Social Security number of a dead person, and Tiffani used one from an old lady in a hospice suffering from mild Alzheimer's."

"Neither of them have any incriminating evidence on you," said Vlad. "Veronica would be implicated in your kidnapping."

"True. But they are hiding. I don't know if they're hiding from fear or planning their next moves."

"I see you're wearing the blue diamond pendant," said Vlad.

"Yes, along with the cross François gave me, it saved my life." I smiled. "Tell me, Vlad, why did you give me this drop of blue vampire blood?"

"In case you need it."

"To become a vampire? I don't think so."

"Remember the devil's skeleton I discovered under the cell in Transylvania many centuries ago?"

I nodded.

"That was a race of an alien species. They lived here on Earth a long time ago, before the giants." Vlad inhaled deeply.

"Giants? What giants?" I asked.

"We are descended from a race of giant humans. They were about ten feet tall or even taller. They were the gods referred to in ancient inscriptions, and they are responsible for genetically creating modern humans."

"Really? And where are they now?"

"They're extinct. The devil race annihilated them."

I was speechless. It sounded so fantastic, but Vlad knew his stuff, and I believed what he said. "Why did the devil annihilate our creators and not us?"

Vlad inhaled deeply as if catching his breath. "Because the giants were very advanced and were the only ones posing a threat to the devils. The giants were not many in number. There was a war, but, in the end, all the giants were killed. Humans, on the other hand, were considered by the devils as mere cattle. You'll find all this information in my library."

"Then the Bible is true. We are the giants' descendants. The gods." I said.

"The Bible, the book of Genesis, is somewhat close to what really happened. In the Bible they're referred to as Nephilims."

"Where did the devils come from?"

"I never found that answer. It could be from right here on Earth, deep inside the Earth. Or from space. The closest place would be the moon or Mars."

Vlad didn't react to the disbelief on my face.

"There is a reason why I asked you about the blue sapphire, and I hope you'll keep wearing it."

"What's that reason, Vlad?"

"The devils may come back. Within your lifetime."

I was stunned at what he said. Those creatures would come back to Earth? "When? And what will happen to humanity?"

"I don't know when. However, that's when Armageddon will happen."

"Armageddon, like in the Bible?"

Vlad nodded his head slowly.

"What was your real intention when you gave me the blue vampire blood pendant?"

"Only vampires will be able to survive the onslaught of the devils."

"Our military will be able to defend the Earth and save humanity."

"I wouldn't be so sure. The giant humans had laser guns and nuclear weapons, and nevertheless they lost."

"Are you saying that I may have to inject the blue blood into my body and become a vampire?"

"You'll have that option. You don't need to do anything about it now, except for one precautionary action."

"What would that be?"

"If someone were to steal the sapphire from you, my entire fake death would have been in vain."

"I'm defenseless. Why did you choose to give it to me?"

"For your protection, in case you need it," repeated Vlad. "And you are not that defenseless."

It was my turn to inhale deeply. "What do you suggest?"

"Implant the sapphire in your body."

I swallowed hard. Place the drop of blue vampire blood in its diamond container in my body? "Wow, that is unexpected. Honestly, it seems like you're trying to make me a vampire."

Vlad looked into my eyes. "I could have made you a vampire the first day I met you. Becoming a vampire is your choice. And I would suggest you do so only when there will be no other course of action."

I ran my fingers through my hair. I was perspiring. "How would this implant work? Who will do it?"

"François."

Chapter 40. The Meeting

"I'll have to think about this, Vlad," I stood up. "I need to go out and meet the lawyers."

"Please consider the implant. It is the safest choice," said Vlad. "Are you going to have your mic on when you talk to the agents?"

"Yes, I will." I gave him a kiss on his forehead and left for the Fifth Avenue Apartment.

"Miss Sanders?" said a dark-haired woman outfitted in a navy-blue business suit and ruffle white blouse. Agents Smith and Johnson flanked her. She showed me her ID badge, fixing me with her stern grey eyes.

"Yes, please come in." I invited the three agents in. "Please follow me." I took them to the living room where my lawyers were waiting. "These are my attorneys, Jennifer Ward and Mark Robertson."

"Nice to meet you." The woman showed her ID badge to them. "I am Special Agent Jane Kelly."

The other two agents showed their badges and introduced themselves as Garry Johnson and Edward Smith. My attorneys scribbled their names on their yellow legal pads and offered their business cards to the agents. We all sat down around the coffee table.

"We'd like to thank you for giving us your time to discuss the circumstances associated with the passing of your great-grandfather," Special Agent Kelly began. "As I mentioned, we will be recording this meeting." She placed a black digital recorder on the coffee table.

"Special Agent Kelly," said my attorney Jennifer Ward. "We are here representing our client Catherina Sanders, and we will be advising her on what questions are prudent to answer or not answer."

"That's fair," said Special Agent Kelly. "We are from the Department of Homeland Security, and we're in the middle of an investigation that involved the late Vlad Draculesti."

"May we know the scope of this investigation?" asked Mark Robertson.

"Mr. Vlad Draculesti was a person of interest to the Department of Homeland Security. That's all we can tell you at this time," she said.

"Was Mr. Draculesti a suspect in a terrorist investigation?"

"We cannot divulge any other details than what I've already said." Special Agent Kelly looked unblinkingly at Mark Robertson.

"Is our client a suspect in your case?" asked Jennifer Ward.

"No. We are searching for answers regarding Mr. Vlad Draculesti," said Special Agent Kelly. "We appreciate your cooperation, Miss Sanders. May we begin?"

And she started asking me questions about Vlad and his death, which I answered. There were not many questions that my attorneys or I objected to answering, even the thornier ones.

"Miss Sanders, you made funeral arrangements at the Souls of God Funeral Home and Mortuary for Mr. Draculesti recently, during the past month – is that correct?" Kelly asked.

"Yes, I did."

"You also made arrangements with Heavenly Bodies Transference to transport the deceased to the mortuary?"

"Yes, I did."

"Did you make reservations with Freedom Helicopter Services, too?"

"Yes."

"Miss Sanders, do you know someone by the name of Antony Sarvis?"

I knew who that was. Mundibuto used that name to make the reservations for the black hearse and the helicopter to JFK. "No, who's he?" I answered with a straight face.

"A person of interest," she said.

"Sorry. I cannot help you with that."

"Miss Sanders, I would like to show you some pictures." Kelly pulled a stack of 8 by 10, black and white photos out of a manila envelope. She showed me the picture of John Miller. "Do you know this man? And if you do, when did you first met him?"

The picture was taken when I had met him with Veronica. Someone had followed us and taken pictures of us. I looked at the photo for some time before I responded. "Miller introduced himself as Veronica Seyler's father. The only time I met him was at Rockefeller Plaza."

"No other times?"

"No."

Special Agent Kelly showed me a picture of Veronica.

"Yes, she is Veronica Seyler. I knew her from Abe Yakowitz's law office. She worked there."

"Did you socialize with her?"

"I went shopping with her and Tiffani Arlin."

"Then I gather that you know her as well." Kelly showed me Tiffani's photo.

"Yes, that is Tiffani Arlin. She worked at the same place with Veronica."

"Have you talked to either one of them since your great-grandfather passed away?"

"No. I'm in mourning. I am in no mood to chat or do anything else."

"Thank you. How about him?" She showed me the picture of François.

"He is François, and I met him recently."

"Are you involved with him?"

"No, I am not."

"Do you have his phone number or address?"

"I know his phone number." I gave them the number of one of his untraced phones, which François did not use any more and had probably smashed and discarded by now.

"Where did you first meet him?"

"In Paris."

"Any other information you can give us about him?"

"That's all."

Special Agent Kelly showed me the picture of a younger man whom I didn't recognize at first. "I don't know who this is."

"Does the name Brenner mean anything to you?"

By the time she asked the question it had occurred to me that it was a younger Miller, or Brenner. Without flinching, I said, "No, nothing."

"Miss Sanders, do you know Dr. Le Bec?"

"Yes. He was Vlad's doctor."

"How many times did you meet him?"

"The only time I met him was when I called him asking for help when my great-grandfather was in bed not responding."

"Can you describe him to us?"

"Describe?" I asked, faking confusion about their request to gain some time to think.

"His physical appearance."

"I see. Well, kind of tall, balding, with a handlebar moustache. He was wearing thick glasses. That's about it."

"Age, hair and eye color, any other significant characteristics?"

"He was middle-aged. Brown, thinning hair. I didn't notice his eye color. I was very upset. I was crying."

"We're sorry for your loss, Miss Sanders. Did you call him on the phone that night?"

"Yes. I have his number on my speed dial."

"Would you mind calling him for us now?"

I raised my eyebrows in surprise. "Sure." I pulled out my phone, searched my contact list, and pressed Dr. Le Bec's number. It rang and then switched me to voicemail. The recorded voice did not belong to François. I left a message.

"May I see your phone, please?" asked Special Agent Kelly. I handed her my bugged phone. "I see you did call Dr. Le Bec."

"Yes."

"Have you talked with Dr. Le Bec since then?"

"No. I've had no reason to."

"Dr. Le Bec signed the death certificate for your great-grandfather, but he doesn't seem to exist."

"What are you saying?" I acted surprised by the news. "I met him and spoke to him. The paramedics and the doorman downstairs spoke to him. What are you implying?"

"We – and now you – can no longer reach this mysterious Dr. Le Bec. He may be an impostor."

"A what? Oh, my God!" I was kind of shocked by their conclusion, although it was true.

"Did your great-grandfather have any life insurance?"

I shrugged. "I don't know if he had life insurance. I haven't checked his legal documents, nor am I of a mind-set to do so anytime soon."

"If you find such policies, be aware that the death certificate has been voided by the New York Office of the Chief Medical Examiner, and no claim can be made on the policy unless this Dr. Le Bec surfaces and it's determined that he is a real doctor. The death of Vlad Draculesti looks suspicious."

"Well, Special Agent Kelly, I've known my long lost great-grandfather for only a short time. I don't know what his life was like or whom he associated with before we knew each other. I never knew Dr. Le Bec, and I only saw him that one time. My great-grandfather said Le Bec was his doctor, and that's all I needed to know. I saw my great-grandfather dead in his bed, I called Dr. Le Bec, and he and the paramedics confirmed he was dead. I carried out his funeral in accordance with his wishes. It may look suspicious to you, but I was there, and it didn't look suspicious to me."

Special Agent Kelly pointed to the urn on the mantle. "Does that urn contain his ashes?"

"Yes."

She looked into my eyes. "Is Mr. Draculesti really dead?"

I straightened up.

"That's a ridiculous question. Cat, you don't have to answer it," said Jennifer Ward.

I stood up. "Can one of you gentlemen bring the urn and place it here on the coffee table?"

Agent Smith stood up and brought the urn to the table.

I unscrewed the lid. "Does this look to you like a live person, Special Agent Kelly?"

The three agents looked inside the urn at the grey ashes and bits of bones.

"If you'll excuse me, I have PMS, and this meeting has just ended."

Chapter 41. The Next Steps

François and Mundibuto returned from upstate New York. Everything was set up in the mountain lodge—a gruesome notion, knowing what we were about to do with Vlad, but according to him, very necessary.

I told everyone about the interrogation, which Angelique and Vlad listened to live.

"You must understand that they have your picture now," I told François

"Yes, but with my dark glasses on," he replied.

"I named you only as François."

"Good. But I'm sure they know my full name. I will not use that name from now on, unless I need to lead them astray. It's a matter of time before they discover that I'm Canadian. That name has run its usefulness. I will start using the name Franc Martineau from now on."

He didn't look like a Franc to me.

"My impression in talking to Homeland Security is that Veronica and Tiffani are nowhere to be found, just as we discovered," I continued. "They have pictures of them, but with sunglasses on. The agents are at a loss because they don't know their real identities. Dr. Le Bec really raised their suspicions because of his absence. It means that either Vlad, or I were involved in faking his existence before your death. They think the motive is to collect on Vlad's life insurance policy."

"Good luck with that. I didn't have any," Vlad said.

"I'm sure they're checking on that detail. And if they don't find insurance policies taken out in your name, the next thing to suspect is that you're not dead," I said.

"After I'm really dead, it will be a non-issue," said Vlad.

"That's true, but, until then, they'll be keeping a keen eye on me. I may be the link to you. I'll just have to be careful."

"If there are no insurance policies under Vlad's name, you're off the hook," said Mundibuto.

"Yes and no," I said. "They know about Vlad, François, Tiffani, Veronica and her so-called dad John Miller, Dr. Le Bec, and me. All, except for me, have disappeared or died like Vlad. I'm the only one around to inherit Vlad's fortune."

François started laughing. "If you would have committed such a crime, you pulled off the crime of the millennium."

"And they have no proof whatsoever," said Vlad. "Unfortunately – and I'm sorry about this – you'll have to get used to being watched by them."

"They don't worry me, and it is better if they watch me," I said, somehow surprised by my newfound courage.

"Why?" Angelique asked.

"Veronica and Tiffani worry me. The Homeland surveillance of me may keep them away."

"That's true," said Angelique.

"The other mystery," I continued, "is how I made arrangements for the funeral and transportation without them knowing."

"Well, you either evaded their surveillance, or someone impersonated you," said Vlad.

"I admitted making the arrangements," I said. "I must have evaded them."

"There are two other exits – no, three – from the Fifth Avenue Apartment building," said Vlad. "The underground garage, the utility entrance, and the refuse access."

"I hope they did not survey those accesses." Then a thought hit me. "Tiffani took the name and social security number of an old woman in a hospice. Who is that woman, and what about her family?"

Just as I finished saying that, François pulled out his laptop and signed on, searching for that name again. "Mundibuto, I think we need to visit this place and check into their files. There is very little information online."

Another break-in, I thought. These vampires were professional thieves, assassins, and impersonators. And I was in it up to my earlobes.

François and Mundibuto left immediately to search for the real Tiffani Arlin.

"It's time for me to retire," said Vlad, and he got up slowly. I took his forearm and helped him to his bedroom. Angelique went up to the Fifth Avenue Apartment to apartment-sit for me.

I helped Vlad get into his bed and tucked him in. "How are you feeling?" I asked him.

"Worse, I'm sorry to say. I have more and more difficulty breathing."

"Vlad, you have so much knowledge. I'm scared of what will happen to me after you're gone."

"Angelique, François, and Mundibuto will help you. They owe me. I cataloged all my experiences, and they are searchable by subject. This information is stored on the same drive as all the other paper documents I have."

"Thanks, but I have another concern to talk to you about. These Strigoi you mentioned."

"What about them?"

"They didn't come to my rescue when I was kidnapped."

Vlad took a few labored breaths. "Did you think of them or ask for their assistance?"

"I'm not sure if I did."

"It may be that they'll become your Strigoi only after I'm dead. I don't know. I will reiterate to them my wish."

"Without your protection, I feel exposed. I don't know how to explain that. Look, even with bodyguards like Jack-Al, things went bad. If it had not been for tracing me by my cross pendant, François could not have rescued me, and I would have been raped and perhaps killed. Definitely killed."

"Certainly. That's why I offered you the blue sapphire pendant."

"Even so, it would take time to become a vampire."

"Not from the drop of blood I gave you."

"What do you mean? You said that it took many, many days to become a vampire when it happened to you."

"Yes, it did. That was because we were exposed to the virus of the devils' decaying blue gel. What you have in there," Vlad pointed at my pendant, "is pure blue blood from me. That stuff will begin working in seconds. Within minutes, your physiology will transform, and you'll become stronger and faster. It will take 24 hours to become a full vampire, with fangs and a thirst for blood. However, you'll be able to defend yourself during that time."

"Another reason to implant the sapphire in my body," I said more to myself.

Vlad nodded. "One more thing. In the Fifth Avenue Apartment, you'll find instructions on how to fry the listening devices installed by the NSA for Homeland Security."

"Fry?"

"Yes, when you want to put an end to their spying."

"Oh, I see. But won't they get suspicious, if I destroy the bugs?"

Vlad laughed softly. "If you do it according to my instructions, it will look like an accident. The frying will happen during a storm, when there is lightning. You flip a switch, and during the next storm – thunderstorms are plentiful in springtime in New York City – the bugs will be smoked. Nothing dangerous, mind you."

"Huh." Vlad had a plan for everything. "Oh, that reminds me. I placed obituaries about your death. The Fifth Avenue Apartment is filling with condolence letters from VIPs, even one from the White House. And, of course, lots of flowers. I got several invitations from eligible bachelors wanting to console me." I sighed. "And the usual pleas to join organizations or make donations."

"You'll do fine, Cat." Vlad patted my hand.

I gave him a kiss on his cheek and left him to sleep.

Chapter 42. Natasha

The next morning, Saturday, we met in the Red Apartment. Mundibuto and François had found some interesting facts about the old woman, the real Tiffani Arlin.

"We visited the hospice last night, and I even talked to the real Mrs. Tiffani Arlin," said François. "She was the governess of the young Tiffani."

"You mean Tiffani's real first name was Tiffani as well?" I asked.

"It is her middle name. Young Tiffani's first name is Natasha, and she is like a daughter to Mrs. Tiffani Arlin. She raised Natasha. While I had a heart-to-heart conversation with the old lady, Mundibuto inspected the files in the office."

"Heh, heh, heh, I'm glad you are sitting down," Mundibuto said. "The hospice is owned by none other than the Hellinherr Institute of Health. She was a lifetime employee of the family, and she's being taken care of by them, by Dr. Hellinherr III himself."

I jumped to my feet.

"Isn't that interesting?" said Vlad.

"Natasha Tiffani Hellinherr is the daughter of Dr. Albert Hellinherr Jr.," said François.

"Junior?" Vlad was surprised. "Dr. Albert Hellinherr Jr. is in his nineties."

We looked at him in confusion.

"I suppose a man in his seventies can have children," said Vlad, shaking his head. "That means Natasha is Hellinherr III's sister. Interesting. Please continue, François."

"The old Tiffani Arlin told me in confidence that Natasha Tiffani wanted all her life to be independent of her father. She wanted to strike out on her own. Natasha Tiffani even told the old woman that she adopted the Arlin name to start a new life."

"Wait a second," I said warily. "What are the chances that Natasha Tiffani ends up working for Abe Yakowitz? Coincidence?"

"Not at all," said Vlad. "Her old man operated from behind the scenes to get her in that office. Why? Maybe because of François or, most likely, me."

"Not me," said François, shaking his head. "I made love to her, and I enjoyed her blood. The bite marks were proof of who I was, but she didn't know that. If her mission was to find me, the Hellinherrs would have come after me in a heartbeat."

"Do you think she ran back to her daddy?" Vlad asked.

"Or her brother," said François. "The old woman was happy because Natasha had reconciled with the family."

"You and I can be identified by her," said Vlad. "After generations of Hellinherrs, the grandson, Hellinherr III, is aware of us and can find out what we look like now."

"That's troublesome," said Angelique.

"Yes, it is," said Vlad. "Obviously, Natasha Tiffani knows my address and yours, François."

"Shoot!" I exclaimed. "I must dispose of the ashes in the urn, in case Hellinherr reads Vlad's obituary and comes to visit."

"Hon, I'll take care of that." Angelique left for the Fifth Avenue Apartment to pour the ashes down a toilet.

"No one can extract DNA from cremated ashes," said François.

"Better not take any chances," said Vlad. "Hellinherr is a genius in genetic biology and chemistry."

"We need to be on guard, especially you, François." I was worried, not so much for Vlad, who was bedridden now and officially dead, but for François, who walked among the living.

"I'll wear a disguise until this ends," said François.

"What if it doesn't end, and it's only just begun?"

-VVV-

Special Agent Jane Kelly sat down, crossed her legs, and looked sternly at Agents Johnson and Smith. "Sit down, gentlemen. We have a lot of work to do here."

The two agents sat down in a circle among the desks. Smith crossed his arms. Johnson crossed his legs, just like Kelly.

"First, let me start on a positive note," said Jane Kelly. "I don't think you were given clear directions on how to approach this investigation. Special Agent Miller gave you instructions and you did as you were told. I am in charge now. We will have to review everything that has happened so far, while monitoring Cat Sanders's whereabouts and conversations."

"Understood," said Agent Smith.

"What is your opinion of what happened?" asked Agent Johnson.

"No opinions, no guesses," said Kelly. "We will determine what happened after we review the facts. Agent Smith, please set surveillance cameras at all possible exits from the building where Cat Sanders resides."

"Yes, ma'am." Smith flinched.

Special Agent Kelly noticed that and raised her eyebrows.

"Special Agent Miller told us not to use titles, just address each other by the last name," clarified Agent Smith.

Kelly found the procedure unusual. "I don't care if we address each other by title or last name when we have discussions. I know you have aliases, being on loan from different intelligence agencies. Jane Kelly is my alias as well. So, relax, use whatever you're comfortable with when we have informal discussions."

"Yes, ma'am," said Agent Smith, divulging his paramilitary background.

"By the way, we are dropping the code names for Dealer and Joker," said Kelly. "We'll call them by their first names, Vlad and Cat."

Johnson and Smith nodded.

"Johnson, I would like you to develop a timeline of events, storyboards with pictures and facts. And a speculations roster," continued Kelly. "You and I will interview all the people Cat and Vlad spoke and met with since the surveillance started. I will go over all the recordings you've made so far. In the meanwhile, we'll keep Agent Pratt in the field, monitoring and following Cat when she's outside the building."

Chapter 43. R.I.P.

Vlad's condition deteriorated fast. I spent all my time with him and slept on an air mattress next to his bed. By the following day, Sunday, he wasn't able to get out of bed. François, Mundibuto, Angelique, and I said our good-byes to him before he lost consciousness. On Monday morning, May 13, he no longer moved. François examined him and declared him dead at noon. He closed Vlad's eyes.

I cried my heart out. I felt so lonely, despite the company of Mundibuto, François, and especially Angelique. She cried, too. I learned that vampires can cry.

It was midafternoon before the first words were spoken.

"Should we cremate him tonight?" wondered François.

"The sooner the better – that's what he would have wished," I said, sniffling from so many shed tears. "I'm going to miss him," I whispered.

"Me, too, hon." Angelique embraced me.

Vlad's body was in the green body bag. We brought him into the great room and placed him on a sofa.

"I'll get the Denali ready," said Mundibuto. "François, would you bring Vlad to the garage?"

"Sure, call me when you're in position," said François.

"Let me set the Fifth Avenue Apartment for no visitors." I left to get everything in order for Vlad's cremation in Upstate New York.

"You know, I should leave through the front door, impersonating you, and lose them," said Angelique.

"That's a good idea," I agreed, and both of us went to the Fifth Avenue Apartment.

By the time I returned to the Red Apartment, François had taken the body down by elevator. I descended to the garage to join them.

Mundibuto was at the wheel, and François was riding shotgun. I climbed in the back seat, while Vlad's body lay in the cargo area. We picked up Angelique a few blocks away, and we left New York, with the agents searching frantically for me.

We drove in silence and, by midnight, we pulled into Vlad's secret lodge. We didn't waste any time. We took the body down to the basement through steel doors.

A yellow metal box, the size of a shipping container, occupied the middle of the basement. It was the incinerator. Electrical conduits, gas pipes, and large air intake and exhaust tubes were connected to it. It did not look like the cremator at the mortuary, but more like an industrial oven of some kind. Mundibuto opened the heavily latched door. There was a secondary door, which opened into the burning chamber. The walls inside were clad in refractory yellow bricks. Even the door to this chamber was lined with bricks. Ceramic nozzles protruded through the floor and the walls. The gas would come from there, and the flames would consume Vlad's body.

Mundibuto unzipped the body bag. Vlad lay in it as serene and white as a ghost. We gathered around him to say our last good-byes. I cried, Angelique cried, and even Mundibuto cried. Angelique and I gave Vlad a last kiss on his cold forehead.

"We'll have to place him on the floor of the incinerator," said François. "The temperature will be so hot that it will melt any metal tray that we may want to use."

Mundibuto took the body in the body bag inside the incinerator and placed him on the brick floor. "Good-bye, massa, and thank you for everything you've done for me." He kneeled before him. By the time he came out, his shoulders were shaking from crying.

François closed the fire chamber door slowly. He paused before closing it completely and took a last look at Vlad Draculesti. The heavy door closed with a metal bang. François pulled the latches closed on the outer door, sealing the door shut. He checked a few gauges, adjusted some mechanical dials, and stepped back, heavy with sorrow. "Good-bye, good old friend," he said.

We stood numb with grief, in total silence.

"We can fire it up any time," said François. "It is set to burn for three hours, at 3,000 degrees Fahrenheit. After that, it may take until noon tomorrow to cool off. Cat, do you want to push the fire ignition button?"

"Me?" I was unsure. "Why don't all four of us push it?"

I stepped close to the incinerator and placed my hand on the red mushroom-head ignition button. Angelique placed her hand on mine, Mundibuto on hers, and François's was last.

"May you rest in peace, Vlad," I said as a final farewell.

I pushed the button while the others pressed on my hand.

The incinerator started with a whining noise before the flames ignited. The needle on a large temperature gauge dial, above the door, climbed fast. François brought four plastic chairs, and we sat in them, looking at the temperature gauge climb.

We talked, remembering stories about Vlad and his life. Angelique knew the most hilarious stories about him. Even I was able to tell a funny story about trying to slash his wrist in a coffee shop. I told them how he convinced me to visit his apartment, and how I discovered that I was his great-granddaughter.

Three hours later, the incinerator shut itself off, and then it began its cooling cycle. We left the basement and went to sleep in the upstairs bedrooms.

Thunder woke me up next morning. I made an effort to remember that I was in the lodge in Upstate New York. I ran to the window to check the weather. Outside it was raining steadily. A storm was advancing from the west toward Manhattan. Loud thunder cracked in the sky. I smirked. I had left the bug-frying button turned on in the Fifth Avenue Apartment. Good-bye bugs! I didn't care what would happen. Vlad was ashes, and no one could bother him any longer.

Angelique was watching the weather on TV when I descended to the first-floor family room. I wasn't hungry, so I made only coffee. Outside it was raining hard.

"Where are the guys?" I asked Angelique.

She turned the TV off. "In the basement, making sure the incinerator is cool enough to open the door."

"Let's go." I grabbed my cup of coffee and went down the stairs, followed by Angelique.

François and Mundibuto were discussing something in front of the incinerator and turned to us, acknowledging our presence.

"Good morning," I said, just to say something, because I didn't feel it was a good morning.

"Morning," said Mundibuto with sad face.

"Cat, we were talking about the biohazard safety of what we may find inside," said François.

"Do you think the fire did not burn it off?"

"We don't know," said Mundibuto.

"What do you suggest?" asked Angelique.

"I'll take a sample and analyze it first," said François. "Therefore, Cat, you'll need to stay away from here."

I didn't want to leave. "Isn't there a gas mask around here?"

"Yes, there are several right here." Mundibuto walked to a metal locker and opened the door. Inside there were gas masks, even rubberized suits.

"How about if I get into one of those?" I pointed to the suits.

Half an hour later, I was encased in a yellow biohazard suit, a bit too large for me, and with a gas mask on. We were ready to open the incinerator. According to the thermometer above the door, the temperature in the chamber was 150 degrees Fahrenheit. Mundibuto opened the outer door and then the fire chamber door. Hot air flooded the basement, and Angelique turned on the exhaust fans. On the floor of the fire chamber lay fine crystalline sand in the shape of a man. That was all that was left of Vlad V, the Vampire.

François had a suit on as well, but no gas mask. He stepped inside cautiously and smelled the air. Although it was hot inside, he didn't seem to mind the heat. Using a small brush, he gathered the ashes – which resembled fine, bluish sand – in a pile and collected it in a sealable glass container, no larger than a medium-sized mayonnaise jar.

He took the container outside and placed it on a nearby workbench. Mundibuto closed the incinerator's doors and latched them. François removed a wooden box from a cabinet and retrieved from it a microscope. He scooped a small sample from the container onto a small rectangular glass slide and placed it under the microscope for inspection. I was getting hot in the rubber suit, but I waited to hear the result. He adjusted the microscope and examined the sample carefully. Then he added a small drop of water in one corner and looked again.

"It is inert." François took his eye off the microscope's eyepiece. "Do you want to see, Cat?"

I nodded and removed my gas mask and the suit. After I was free of the cumbersome attire, I looked through the microscope. In the dry portion of the slide I saw tiny blue crystals surrounded by many white crystals and a very few black micro-grains. The wet side was the same, except the black particles floated in the water.

"How do you know it's inert?" I asked François.

"There is nothing moving, no reactions, nothing is dissolving, among other things I can discern about it. It is crystalline in nature, baked to a crisp."

"What am I seeing?"

"The blue crystals are what's left of the vampire blood. The white crystals are the bones and flesh, and everything else you see is from the clothes and the bag." François gave me a quick smile of encouragement. "It's safe."

"Why are so few ashes left, unlike the other body?" I asked.

"A higher burning temperature, and I suspect that some of the vampire bio-composition may have been combustible as well."

After Mundibuto and Angelique satisfied their curiosity by looking through the microscope, François poured the sample back into the glass container, sealed it, and gave it to me. I cradled the warm glass container in my arms, close to my heart. Mundibuto fired up the incinerator and turned the interior exhaust fans on to purge the last remains of Vlad's ashes.

Upstairs, I placed the glass container in my bag. I felt comforted by it, knowing that it contained the remains of Vlad. And soon we were back on the rainy expressway to Manhattan.

It was Tuesday in the late evening when we returned to the safe houses. I left the glass container in Vlad's bedroom in the Red Apartment, and I returned to the Fifth Avenue Apartment through the front entrance. Angelique was waiting for me there, just in case there was an unexpected surprise in the apartment. Everything was quiet. Only the grandfather clock was ticking.

I checked the security status on the laptop, and everything checked green. The bugs were fried. "We can talk now," I told Angelique.

"Would you like me to stay with you here for a while?" she asked me.

"Oh, that would be great." I was glad for her offer. I would have felt very lonely by myself. "You can take any bedroom you want."

"I'll take the one close to the Red Apartment access," she said.

"Thank you for staying with me." My stomach growled. I headed for the kitchen. "I need to eat something. Help yourself to drinks."

It was all over. Vlad was dead, and his ashes were secure in a sealed container in the safe. No one could bother him now.

Mundibuto was the first to leave. He promised he would keep in touch. François left a few days later, but he promised to return in early June. Angelique agreed to stay with me for a month. I so appreciated her company. Agent Pratt kept watch on my apartment, and Angelique took a liking to him, visiting him in his hotel room just about every night. Poor Agent Pratt – he had no idea whom he was sleeping with. He probably screamed with pleasure and for mercy while she was sucking him dry, if you know what I mean.

Homeland Security did not make any other attempts to bug my apartment, from what I could tell. They just observed me.

Chapter 44. The Puzzle

"Special Agent Jane Kelly speaking."

"Ma'am, this is Agent Smith. We lost audio from Vlad's apartment."

"Get Johnson on a three-way call."

"He's right here with me. Let me put you on speaker."

"Did Cat ever come home after we lost her late yesterday afternoon?" asked Kelly.

"Yes, she just returned tonight," answered Johnson.

"Any idea about Cat's whereabouts for the past 24 hours?" Kelly asked.

"No, sorry, not a sign," said Johnson.

"What else?"

"The reason I called you is because we've lost audio from her apartment," said Smith.

"Do we know why, Smith?"

"Yes," said Smith. "The storm. The lightning fried our listening devices."

"How could this happen?"

"They were grounded, and the electrical discharge zapped them," said Smith. "We need to replace the burned ones with new devices."

"Lightning is not rare in New York City," said Kelley.

"We'll replace them with battery powered devices," said Smith.

"Not yet. Wait until I get back to you."

Special Agent Kelly and Agents Smith and Johnson reconvened in the Homeland Security office in Manhattan to review the status of their operation.

"Smith, please update us on the surveillance cameras," said Kelly.

"We've installed several cameras around the suspect's domicile, ma'am," said Smith. "We have two cameras pointed at the front entrance of the building, a camera at the utility exit, one pointing at the refuse alley, and another one in the underground garage. Five cameras, covering all the exits. We still have a camera installed on the light pole right across the avenue, pointing at the apartment's terrace. It also contains a directional microphone. The NSA set up a 24/7 survey team to monitor the cameras and audio we receive from the apartment's internal mics, if we replace them. Should we replace them?"

"No," said Kelly. "Now that Vlad's ashes are supposedly resting in a bronze urn on the mantle, let's give Cat a sense of assurance that we've given up surveying her. In other words, let's monitor her very discreetly."

"Very well," said Smith.

"Good. Any movements or communications by phone or Internet in the meanwhile?"

"No. Cat hasn't left the building. She seems to be in seclusion," said Smith. "She made some phone calls, mostly for takeout food. Nothing out of the ordinary."

"OK," said Kelly. "Johnson and I will continue interviewing people who spoke with Cat and Vlad. And I'm listening to the recordings."

"Just as Cat told us, she is the one who visited and talked to all the people at the church and funeral home, and made the arrangements," said Johnson. "I'm baffled at how she eluded our surveillance."

"It's the end of May," Kelly sighed. "Johnson, I see you set up several boards for the events timeline."

"A few interesting details surfaced." Johnson stood up and walked to the boards. "Do you want an overview or details?"

"Overview," said Kelly.

"An overview will be good," Smith agreed.

"Very well." Johnson cleared his throat. He pointed to the pictures on the first board. "It started with the Homeland Security supercomputer identifying Vlad Draculesti as a person of interest because of his longevity and perpetual youth. That is no longer true, because he got old and allegedly died. Additional evidence to justify the investigation was provided by a surveillance video, which showed Vlad Draculesti pushing two robbers. The two became airborne and flew twenty-some feet, crashing into a back wall.

"Soon after we started our investigation, we learned that Vlad and Cat had visited Abe Yakowitz's law firm. After which, Cat went shopping in several stores in Manhattan, accompanied by Veronica Seyler and Tiffani Arlin. A few days later, Cat flew to Geneva, Liechtenstein, and Paris. In Geneva and Liechtenstein, she visited several banks and financial institutions. In Paris, she shopped. The Interpol agents did not see anything suspicious in her activities, and she did not meet anyone else, other than the bank employees and the sales people in the Paris stores she was shopping in. Special Agent Miller told us that he had a source who informed him that Cat had become Vlad's heiress."

"Who was the source?" asked Kelly.

"He never divulged the informant's name to us," said Smith.

"In light of our recent discussion with Cat, Veronica Seyler should be that suspect," added Johnson.

"If what Cat said about the relationship of Miller and Seyler is true," Jane Kelly stood up and walked to the board, "then could we have a father-daughter team acting independently for their own gain?"

Johnson and Smith exchanged mystified looks.

"I'll add that as an issue." Johnson scribbled on the board. "Although, after we learned that Miller was Brenner, we checked his background but found no offspring, just three broken marriages."

"And a history of alcoholism," said Smith. "A rumor that somehow followed him even under the alias John Miller."

"A drunk." Kelly made a note. "We need to do a deeper investigation into Brenner. Continue, Johnson."

"The evening Joker returned to New York from her European trip, she moved in with Dealer."

"That hurriedly?" questioned Kelly. "As a note, after reviewing that segment of the recordings, I found no preparatory reason why she did that. Something caused that impetuous decision."

"Us?" wondered Smith.

"You may have a point there, Smith," said Jane Kelly. "Listening to the recorded conversations there were a lot of vague discussions, but nothing of significance. We could infer that they were made aware of the bugs."

"By whom?" Smith wondered, furrowing his eyebrows.

"We'll circle back to that. Go on, Johnson." Kelly made another note.

"Vlad and Cat took walks in Central Park in the late evenings. They met no other people. Without us being aware of it, Cat visited the New Age Eastern Church and inquired about becoming a member. On the same day, she visited the Souls of God Funeral Home and Mortuary in Brooklyn and purchased a pre-need funeral package. She spared no expense to have an expeditious funeral for her great-grandfather."

"That's the church doctrine, expeditious cremation," said Smith.

"Dispose of the body ASAP," commented Kelly, tapping her chin with her pen. And she added more notes in her book.

Johnson and Smith nodded.

"It was express-lane cremation," said Smith.

"By the way," said Johnson. "According to the recordings, Cat was in her apartment during the time of the visits to the church and funeral home."

"Yes, I verified that, too," said Kelly.

"The reservation for the hearse with Heavenly Bodies Transference was made by phone by Cat. We have no recording of that conversation from her tapped phone, nor of subsequent conversations with the funeral home. It was done on an untraced cell phone outside the apartment."

"So she had another, clean cell phone or an accomplice posing as her," said Kelly. "Or she left pre-recorded voices in the apartment and went out undetected to make funeral arrangements. Why the secrecy?"

"The express-lane cremation could have been interrupted, if we knew her plans," speculated Smith.

"Possibly," agreed Johnson. "Anyway, she managed to evade our detection during the Rockefeller Plaza outing, and she evaded us purposely. We didn't know about that outing until we saw the pictures taken of them. Now I have a question of my own, Kelly. Why were those photos taken?"

"I took them," said Jane Kelly. "John Miller – Brenner – was a suspect."

"No way!" Smith was surprised by the news.

"I'm not surprised." Johnson nodded, as if his suspicion was confirmed.

Smith and Kelly stared at Johnson.

"His behavior somehow made me distrust him," Johnson said.

"Good nose, Johnson," said Kelly. "Assistant Deputy Director Jaworski got a tip from Homeland Internal Affairs about some improprieties associated with Brenner. Also, it was not the supercomputer that initiated the search on Vlad Draculesti. The supercomputer doesn't do that. It was Brenner who prompted the search."

"No sh–" Johnson stopped short.

"No shit it is, Johnson," said Kelly without embarrassment. "Brenner was the last agent in the FBI who investigated Dealer. He had a personal motive to investigate Vlad Draculesti again."

"That's why the name of the last agent working on the case was deleted," said Smith. "Miller didn't want us to know who the last investigating agent was."

"By the way," Johnson said, as his eyes widened. "The previous two FBI agents working on the Draculesti case died of heart attacks. Didn't they, Smith?"

"Yes, that's true," said Smith. "Rod Tiller and Frank Hulbert. What are the chances that Vlad somehow killed them?"

"Do you think Brenner knew that?" wondered Johnson.

"Another enigma," said Jane Kelly, and she added more notes. "Anyway, I was assigned to trail Miller-Brenner. I followed him to Rockefeller Center and, as luck would have it, I found most of the players in one place. Other than Cat and Miller-Brenner, we didn't know and still don't know the real identities of the others. Yet. Continue, Johnson."

"Well, afterward, Vlad and Cat visited the church, and Dealer converted. He gave a generous donation. Then everything goes quiet for a few days, during which Miller went missing. Cat left the apartment on Friday morning, May 3rd, going shopping, and we lost her. She came back early midafternoon, and found Vlad unconscious. She called Dr. Le Bec and then the paramedics. Soon after, Vlad was pronounced dead.

"Smith and I followed the black hearse, which, we now suspect, was a decoy, while Vlad's body was loaded later into a white hearse and subsequently onto the helicopter. Cat and her escort took the helicopter to Dyker Beach Park in Brooklyn and went to the funeral home, where Vlad was expeditiously cremated.

"The reservations for the black hearse and another helicopter to fly to JFK were made under the name Anthony Sarvis, and payment was made with a credit card issued to an Anthony Sarvis of Queens. This man is retired, living on a social security check, and he had no idea that he had a credit card. His stolen ID was used to obtain the card. There was no corpse at JFK to be picked up by the black hearse, and the helicopter's flight to JFK was cancelled later that day. By then Vlad's body was just ashes in an urn."

"Thank you, Agent Johnson," Kelly said. "As you know, Cat admitted to having made the arrangements for the funeral and transportation. It could have been her or an accomplice posing as her. If that's the case, we have another possible suspect, a Cat look-alike who did it all." She made more notes.

"What do we know so far?" Kelly continued. "Miller may have had an ulterior motive to investigate Vlad, and it is highly probable that he informed Vlad of the ongoing surveillance on his apartment. Being aware of that, Vlad and Cat played along. Miller must have known something very damaging about Vlad, and Vlad decided to fake his own death with the help of Cat and other accomplices."

"You mean Cat did not kill Vlad to get his money?" Johnson said.

"Why would she do that?" questioned Kelly. "She was his heiress already."

"That's true," agreed Smith. "The money was hers."

"As far as we can tell, we have three parties involved in this." Jane Kelly raised one finger. "First, the US Department of Homeland Security and the NSA. That's us. Tom Brenner, alias John Miller, initiated the investigation on Vlad Draculesti, and the scope of the investigation was the longevity of Vlad Draculesti."

She raised a second finger. "Second, Miller-Brenner and possibly his alleged daughter, Veronica Seyler, were working under the umbrella of Homeland Security. His motive could have been blackmail. Money. Miller didn't want Vlad Draculesti to be exposed before he achieved his goal. He warned Draculesti of the surveillance, therefore the investigation dragged on, giving Miller time to act on his personal plan."

Jane Kelly raised a third finger. "Third, Vlad Draculesti and Catherina Sanders are the suspects.

Draculesti's motive is to remain undiscovered and keep his secret a secret. Cat Sanders could be his great-granddaughter, or he could have hired her to help him out. Her motive is money or to benefit from Draculesti's secret. Rather than be discovered, Vlad Draculesti resolved to fake his own death, and Cat Sanders helped him. I think Vlad Draculesti is alive and well, and, by now, living abroad."

"Then who died, and who was cremated as Vlad Draculesti?" wondered Johnson.

"What is Draculesti's secret?" asked Smith.

"Yes, two unknowns. Who was the dead person, and what was Vlad's secret?" said Kelly. "Let's start with his secret. The scope of the investigation was Vlad Draculesti's longevity. What did he do to stay young for so long?"

"You know we speculated that he may be a vampire," said Johnson doubtfully.

Jane Kelly wrote on the board. "Vampire. Possible? Let's suppose that he did something with human blood to maintain his youth. That's a possibility. What else?"

"Alien," said Smith.

"Alien, from Earth or otherwise." Kelly wrote on the board. "I would sooner buy the vampire version, but alien is a remote possibility as well."

"Remember the force with which he shoved the muggers?" said Johnson.

"Secret powers." Kelly added it to the board. "The Pentagon and Homeland Security would really be interested in this aspect. What else?"

"Tiller and Hulbert both died of heart attacks," said Smith. "Could Vlad Draculesti have killed them? And how about Miller-Brenner? Did he know that and want to use it against Vlad?"

"That's a motive, to fake your own death and escape prosecution," Kelly said and wrote it on the board. "If you can think of another reason, let me know, otherwise I'll write 'others'."

Smith and Johnson shook their heads.

"OK, back to Miller-Brenner," said Kelly. "What was he doing? And what happened to him?"

"He may be dead," said Johnson. "I think Vlad Draculesti and his accomplices killed him, and possibly Veronica Seyler and Tiffani Arlin, and then faked his own death."

"Besides finding Vlad Draculesti, we need to find Miller-Brenner or find out what happened to him," said Kelly. "We need to find the other two women, the real Veronica Seyler and Tiffani Arlin. Also, François Le Beau and Dr. Le Bec. Meanwhile, Cat Sanders is our only link to Vlad Draculesti, François Le Beau, and Dr. Le Bec."

"The question is, who did Cat cremate, if the stiff was not Vlad Draculesti?" asked Johnson.

"And who really is this Cat Sanders?" added Smith. "So versatile and cunning, as if she were trained by the CIA."

"Maybe," said Kelly. "Because of all the incongruities and missing persons, we are going on the premise that Vlad did not die and used a look-alike to kill and cremate. When was the last time you saw Miller-Brenner?"

"I saw him last, and I made a declaration about that fact," said Smith. "He was tense, and he left the office for a smoke sometime after 10 pm on Wednesday, May 1st. That is the last I saw of him. The security camera showed him exiting onto the side street, and the exact time of exit was recorded by the camera."

"And when did you notice his absence?" asked Kelly.

"Well, Johnson was the first to ask for him the next day before noon," said Smith.

Johnson nodded. "We tried calling him, sent messages, but he never responded. After lunch we called the main office and informed them about him not answering our calls. An agent was sent to his hotel, but he wasn't there. The main office started an investigation by 5 pm, and soon after they called in the FBI."

"Two days later they found his car in a garage on 40th. Spotless," Smith said.

Jane Kelly thought for a moment. "Unless he wanted to fake his own death or disappearance, just like Vlad, he wouldn't have cleaned his car. The more I think about this, the more I believe Brenner was killed."

"And his body?" wondered Johnson. "The river?"

"Here we are trying to investigate Vlad Draculesti, and we're investigating Tom Brenner," said Kelly, shaking her head. "We need to find the other players. Smith, please let the FBI know to intensify their search into the identities of François Le Beau, Dr. Le Bec, Veronica Seyler, and Tiffani Arlin." Kelly thought for a moment. "And a worldwide search for Vlad Draculesti. Let Interpol look for him, especially in Romania."

Artist sketches were rendered for Veronica Seyler and Tiffani Arlin with the help of Abe Yakowitz's employees.

"The FBI found that both their names were assumed identities," said Jane Kelly. "The name Veronica Seyler belonged to a dead person. The real Tiffani Arlin was an old woman, who just died in a hospice. The supercomputer hasn't identified the two real persons yet. When we find them, I think that those two would shed a lot of light on what happened."

"Tiffani Arlin died of natural causes?" Johnson asked.

"She died of a heart attack on May 15th," said Kelly.

"Another one dying of a heart attack," Smith said.

"But she was an old woman with Alzheimer's," said Kelly.

"We found François Le Beau," said Johnson, beaming. "He's a French national, good-looking devil." Johnson displayed a picture of him on his computer to show Special Agent Kelly and Agent Smith. "He recently immigrated to Canada, and he resides in Montreal. We have agents trying to find him. They even entered his apartment, but he seems to have fled."

"He is gorgeous," agreed Kelly. "Did you get the supercomputer to identify him?"

"I did," said Johnson, with a smile a mile wide. "They found a picture of him in 1908 at the Sorbonne in Paris. He was on the faculty as a professor of anatomy and medical sciences."

"And?" asked Kelly.

"He looks the same," said Johnson. "As youthful as Vlad Draculesti used to look."

"These people have found the fountain of youth," commented Smith.

"Remember when we first speculated that Vlad was a vampire?" said Johnson.

"Vlad the Impaler – Dracula." Smith smirked.

"That would have been farfetched when you started the case," said Kelly. "However, with this fellow and his picture from 1908, vampire may make sense, or something else that maintains these men's youth. Good job, Johnson."

"Canadian law enforcement found Dr. Le Bec!" Johnson was jubilant a day later. "Dr. Frank Le Bec of Montreal, Canada. He has been on sabbatical since April and is with Doctors without Borders until September. This is his photo."

Smith and Kelly stared at the picture on the screen of a forty-something, blond, blue-eyed man.

"He doesn't look like the man Cat, the paramedics, and the doorman described," said Smith. "Besides, this doctor was on a ship somewhere off the coast of Africa when Vlad died."

"An impostor took his identity," said Kelly. "Johnson, let's inquire if he knows François Le Beau."

The next day, they received a message from the real Dr. Le Bec acknowledging that he knew a François Le Beau from Montreal. He also identified Le Beau from the picture sent to him.

"François Le Beau had a medical background," said Kelly. "What if Le Beau impersonated Dr. Le Bec?"

"That could be," agreed Johnson.

"In that case, François Le Beau is our sole suspect and not Le Bec," said Smith. "This narrows down the list somewhat."

Special Agent Kelly removed her earphones and stood up abruptly. "Smith, Johnson!" she called the agents who were in the office with her. "Listen to this."

She pushed the play button on her computer screen and increased the volume. "Hey, Cat, this is Veronica. How would you like to go out and have a drink? It's hump day. Call me."

"Did you ever hear this message?" Kelly asked.

"Yes," said Smith. "She never returned the call . . . " His voice trailed off, realizing that Cat may have returned the call on another, untraced phone.

"What if she called back?" Jane Kelly asked, raising her eyebrows. "What if she went out with Veronica?"

Agent Smith pecked on his computer keyboard. "The call was made on Wednesday, May 1st, at 8:32 pm. The audio from the apartment didn't record her phone ringing at the time. She is chatting with Vlad. Nonsenses as usual. Maybe the ring tone was off?"

"No sign of her exiting the building from that time until Friday morning," said Johnson, reading the surveillance roster.

"What if she did and evaded us altogether?" Kelly pursed her lips. "What if Veronica was setting a trap for her, and she took the bait?"

"A trap? What for?" asked Johnson.

"A blackmailer uses all the tools available," said Kelly. "We know that Miller was known to Veronica. We don't know if he was known by the name of Brenner as well. What if Miller asked Veronica to entice Cat to leave her apartment?"

"To kidnap her?" Johnson jumped to his feet.

"But Cat wasn't kidnapped," Smith said. "We know that."

"When did Miller go missing?" Kelly asked, looking at them sideways.

"Holy shit!" shouted Smith, and he flushed red. "The last time I saw him was that Wednesday evening at about 10 pm. The same evening that Veronica wanted to go out drinking with Cat."

"And we noticed Miller's absence on Thursday, the next day." Johnson sat down slowly. "This is unreal."

"Imagine that Miller planned to kidnap Cat, using Veronica as bait," said Kelly. "The plan went astray, and Vlad nabbed Miller instead. Cat returns home safe and sound without us knowing any different."

"Vlad did Miller in," said Johnson. "No doubt about it."

"And where is Miller's body now?" asked Smith.

Kelly walked to the timeline board. She removed Miller's photo and placed it side by side with Vlad's. "What do you think?"

Smith and Johnson approached and stared intensely.

"They kind of look alike." Johnson swallowed hard. "Both white males, sixtyish, hair combed back, white at the temples for Miller, and completely white for Vlad. Narrow noses. But the eyes are not the same. Miller's are hazel, Vlad's are brown."

"A dead man's eyes are closed," said Kelly. "Nobody notices the eye color."

"Are you saying that Miller was cremated instead of Vlad Draculesti?" Smith asked. "The ashes we saw in the urn were Miller's?"

"And we will never be able to prove it," concluded Kelly. "They pulled off the perfect crime."

"How about the ashes?" Smith asked.

"Even if the ashes still exist, no evidence can be extracted from them," said Kelly.

"Wow, wow, wow!" exclaimed Smith. "How were they able to plan such a crime? Cat must be CIA."

"I inquired. No such connection," Kelly said. "But Vlad and Cat and other accomplices know what happened. Unfortunately, we only have Cat to ask questions of, and we have no proof of what she did."

"What if we trace Cat's movements on the night of Wednesday, May 1st?" proposed Johnson.

"Cabs, limo services?" Smith asked.

"Let's do that," agreed Kelly.

The following day, the results came in. "No cab or limo service was called to that address between

8:30 pm and midnight on that Wednesday," said Smith.

"Vlad and Cat traveled in New York by limo mostly." Johnson tapped on his computer. "They used Regency Manhattan Limousine Services. I'll give them a call."

"You know they used bodyguards as well." Smith accessed his computer.

Kelly watched them with her arms folded, hopeful.

"No luck," said Johnson. "There was no limo requested from Regency Manhattan Limo on that evening to that address. But one of their limos was stolen and has been missing since that Wednesday night. On their surveillance camera, they saw the limo going out the gates, but the driver could not be identified. They think it was an inside job. They have a suspect, one of their chauffeurs by the name of Mathew Green. He cannot be found."

"What do you know?" said Smith, shaking his head. "Listen to what I just found out about the bodyguards Draculesti usually hired."

"I get a sense that the plot is thickening," said Kelly.

"Vlad Draculesti had an account with VIP Bodyguards and Security Services," said Smith. "His preferred bodyguards were Al Patterson and Jack McLoyd. And they have been missing since Thursday, May 2nd. That's when they were supposed to report back for work."

"Isn't that interesting?" said Kelly. "The usual limo and bodyguards Draculesti uses go missing."

"Do you think Vlad Draculesti killed them, too?" asked Johnson.

"Or Miller."

"To get rid of the accomplices who helped him kidnap Cat," said Kelly.

"I hope it stops here," said Johnson.

A few days later, Johnson saw breaking news popping up on the flat panel TV on the office wall. He quickly placed his cup of coffee on the desk and shouted to Smith, who was in the office, to watch. A salvage barge was pulling a limo from the East River.

"They found the limo," said Special Agent Kelly, entering the office.

"Yes, it's on TV." Johnson pointed to the screen.

"Anyone inside?" Smith asked.

"It hasn't been announced on the news, but they found three bodies in the trunk," said Kelly. "The limo belongs to Regency Manhattan Limousine Services. The NYPD will need to check DNA to identify the bodies."

"Anyone want to bet that the three aren't the chauffeur and the bodyguards?" Johnson asked.

"If you give me a thousand to one, I'll bet you a dollar," said Smith.

Kelly shook her head. "Let's wait and find out what clues they discover from the bodies." She read her text message. "This is gory, but one of the bodies was decapitated. And they found heavy chains in the trunk as well."

"Someone was into S&M," smirked Johnson.

"NYPD forensics has identified the bodies in the limo," said Johnson. "They are who we suspected them to be."

Smith looked through the pictures the NYPD provided and read the causes of death issued by the coroner. "This Mathew fellow seems to have been smashed against a wall." He frowned. "Johnson, does it sound similar to what Vlad did to the muggers on the video?"

"Yeah," agreed Johnson. "Just about every bone is broken in his body. The coroner stipulates that he may have been dropped from a third-story height. The similarities are there."

"Who could have ripped off this other guy's head?" wondered Smith.

"They found teeth marks on his neck." Johnson read the report. "The marks resemble tiger fangs." Johnson exchanged concerned looks with Smith.

"Al Patterson, the black guy, seemed to have fared better than the other two," said Smith, looking at the report on his screen. "He died from a broken neck, no fang marks on him."

"But both he and McLoyd had cracked skulls," said Johnson. "My God, what happened to those three?"

"Who killed them so savagely?" Kelly came into the office asking the relevant question.

"Who else but Vlad?" Smith said.

"There is proof of how violent Vlad Draculesti and his gang can be," said Kelly.

"Shouldn't we inform the NYPD about our suspicions?" Johnson asked.

"What good will that do them?" said Kelly. "We want to keep this quiet and give Cat Sanders the impression that things have returned to normal."

Chapter 45. On My Own

It was June, and Vlad had been gone for almost three weeks by then. François came back, as he had promised. I had missed him, and he looked as delightful to the eye as ever, although in public he wore a longish white wig and a goatee, trying to pass as an old hippie. Even then, women turned their heads to look at him. I think it was his cute butt.

I gave him a big hug, and he gave me a good squeeze, too.

"Cat, beware," he told me. "They found that my identity goes back to France, early in the last century."

"Oh, no!" I cried.

"It's alright. I've disappeared, and they don't know where to find me."

"But, François, they have your picture now."

"Yes, and knowing that, I took defensive measures. I abandoned all my previous residences. I live in the US now, and I wear disguises when I'm in public."

"I'm sorry you got involved in this mess." And I was really sorry.

"It was a matter of time. Like Vlad said, the supercomputers are hard at work cataloguing every person in this country and elsewhere. But no need to worry."

I had to do something about the blue sapphire. Now that François was back, I visited him in the Green Apartment.

"François, I have a favor to ask."

"Anything, Cat."

"Vlad gave me this blue sapphire." I lifted the pendant with a finger. "Do you know what this is?"

"Vampire blood."

"You know. Good. Vlad told me that the safest place for it would be implanted in my body."

"I agree."

"Would you implant it, please?"

François stood still and looked at me with his deep blue eyes. "Behind the left or right ear?"

"Right. I use the phone on the left."

"When would you like me to implant it?"

"Right now. And one more thing."

"Yes?"

"In case I need it, how do I break the diamond container?"

He came close to me, placed his hands behind my neck, and unclasped the chain. As he stood there in front of me, I was so tempted to put my arms around him, but this was serious business, so I abstained. He removed the gem, and he twisted both ends. The outer diamond was a container, and lodged inside was the *blue sapphire*. Inside it was another diamond shell, much smaller, which contained the blue vampire blood. He held the small ampule between his thumb and index finger. "This is a container made of two diamonds. They will open when you press them together at the extremities, just as I'm holding it right now."

"Huh! Wicked! But will I be able to do that once it is in my body?"

"Oh, yes. I'll insert it in such a way that by using your right thumb and index finger, you can squeeze it when needed. I hope you won't have to do that."

"Why not?"

"Certain things and feelings will not be the same as they were when you were a human. Others things will be better. Then, you won't die. But that's not the worst part. The worst part is when you love someone, and she or he ages and dies, and you're left behind, all alone."

I threw my arms around him and began to cry. He held me, consoling me. "I miss Vlad," I said between sobs.

"Me, too, *ma chérie*."

My crying slowly abated. I felt embarrassed.

"Why don't you go and wash your face, and behind your right ear as well."

I did as instructed and returned. François brought out his medical bag, opened it, and pulled a small syringe from it. I held my earlobe down, and he rubbed alcohol on the insertion spot.

"You'll feel a prick from the injection needle. This will numb you." As he said that he injected me.

"Ouch!" I said.

"That was the worst part." François smiled at me like a doctor smiles at a little girl. And at that moment I felt like a little girl.

He placed the diamond ampule with the vampire blood in a small alcohol container, then removed it and placed it on gauze. I looked away as he brought the scalpel behind my ear. Not that I could see anything, but instinct told me what he did. He made the incision behind my ear. It didn't hurt, but I felt the pressure.

Expertly he inserted the blue sapphire behind my right ear and taped the incision closed. He did not use stitches.

"Fantastic!" He looked proudly at me.

I touched the area behind my ear and felt the small bump beneath the tape, where the blue sapphire was lodged. I gave François a big hug and a kiss on the cheek. "Anything else I need to do, Dr. François?"

"No, you're good. Don't wash that part of your body for a couple of days. It will feel like a large grain of rice, located between your ear and skull. Do you remember how to open it?"

I nodded, and I mimicked pinching the ends of the blue blood vial with my fingers.

"Excellent!" He patted me on my tush. Shamelessly, I didn't mind.

François left again the next day, and Angelique departed for Rio a few days later. I felt lonely, but I immersed myself in the tons of information Vlad had accumulated, and time passed quickly. François promised he would return to visit me at the end of June. I hoped he'd keep his promise.

-VVV-

"June's almost over, and no sign of Vlad anywhere in the world." Special Agent Jane Kelly sighed. "No helpful clues from the limo, other than that the three bodies belonged to Al Patterson, Jack McLoyd, and Mathew Green." Kelly scratched her head. "I listened and re-listened to the recordings and churned over all the facts, but I don't see anything new."

"Did you talk to Agent Pratt?" asked Smith. "He kept most of the watch on the apartment."

"Sure, in the first days when I took over the case." Kelly paused. "Except for one thing – the pictures from Rockefeller Center. I never showed those pictures to him or all the other agents who kept watch on the apartment."

"I'll take this task and see what they say," said Johnson. He transmitted the pictures to the agents. "What do you know? Pratt is in the building. I'll ask him to come over."

"How are you, Agent Pratt?" Kelly greeted him.

"Very well, thanks, Special Agent Kelly," answered the young agent. "There's nothing suspicious to report from the Fifth Avenue location." He nodded toward Johnson and Smith as a salute.

"Thanks, but this is not why we want to talk to you. Have a seat," said Kelly. She opened a large manila envelope and pulled a stack of photos out. "These pictures were taken at Rockefeller Center. Tell us if you can identify any of these people." Kelly placed Miller and Cat's pictures on the desk.

"Joker – Cat Sanders – and Special Agent Miller," said Pratt, blushing. "I wasn't aware Joker was there, and with Miller, too."

"Don't worry about that." Kelly placed Veronica and Tiffani's pictures on the desk.

Pratt shook his head. "I don't know who they are."

Kelly showed him François Le Beau's picture.

"Never saw him," said Pratt.

"Well, it was worth a try." Kelly placed the photos on the stack of other pictures. She went to insert them back into the envelope, but they were misaligned. As she tried to force them in, the pictures instead fanned out and spilled onto the desk and the floor.

Pratt bent down to help collect the pictures, and he stood up, holding one of the pictures. It was one of the panoramic photos taken that day. He stared intently at the picture and paled.

"What's the matter, Agent Pratt?" asked Kelly.

Pratt took a moment before speaking. "I think I know this woman." He pointed to a woman in one corner of the plaza. "Although I'm not sure."

"This one?" asked Smith, pointing to the woman.

Pratt nodded.

"We've got color versions of this in the computer," said Smith. He pulled up the picture on the screen and zoomed in on the woman. She was a red-haired, attractive woman, dressed in dark slacks and jacket. Large sunglasses covered her eyes. Smith zoomed in on her head. "Do you know her, Pratt?"

"I do. Her name is Angelique. What was she doing there?"

"Why? Wasn't this Angelique supposed to be there?" asked Smith.

"No, I didn't meant that," said Pratt. "What are the chances that a woman I've met recently ends up in this investigation's photos?"

"Who's she?" asked Kelly.

"A woman I befriended recently," said Pratt.

"Did you have an affair with her?" Kelly asked.

Pratt looked away. "Yes. I did."

"What's her last name? Where does she live?"

"I don't know. I haven't seen her in a couple of weeks."

"Did you call her?"

"No, I've never talked to her by phone. She tells me when she'll see me again, or she just meets me without announcement."

"Where did you meet her? Where were you seeing her?"

"I met her at a coffee shop, and we hit it off. After that, she visited me in my hotel room." Pratt swallowed.

"Maybe it was a coincidence that the person you were involved with sexually was there at the time," said Kelly.

Pratt shrugged, but he wasn't so sure.

"That's no coincidence," said Johnson, who, in the meantime, was fingering though the rest of the photos. "She appears in this photo, too. And she definitely was watching Cat when she was at the table with Veronica and Miller, and, in this one, she's watching François Le Beau while he was arguing with Tiffani."

"Take a look at this." Smith pointed to a magnified picture of Angelique. "This, here on the collar, looks like a mini-mic."

"Who is she, Pratt?" Kelly asked again.

"That's all I know," said Pratt, now concerned for his job.

"Well, if she's not from another agency, I'd say from the looks of it she may be part of Vlad and Cat's gang," said Kelly. "Pratt, do you remember her well enough to describe her features for a sketch artist?"

"Yes, I think so," said Pratt. "I have no idea who she is."

"Don't worry," said Kelly. "I'm glad you recognized her."

"This could be Cat's double," Smith smiled. "One more suspect close to being identified."

Johnson approached Pratt. "I'll go with you to the rendering artist to put together her picture. But before that I have a, a kind of tacky question to ask you."

"Sure, go ahead," said Pratt.

"You had sex with her, right?"

Pratt nodded, averting his eyes.

"Anything unusual about her? Any marks she left on your body?" Johnson asked.

Kelly was about to interject, but she saw Pratt's stunned face. "How do you know?"

"I don't – tell us about that," said Johnson.

"Every time I slept with her I got hickeys, mostly on my neck."

-VVV-

One night, I needed to use the bathroom, and, as I was returning, half asleep, to my bed, I stubbed my toe on a chair leg. I jumped on the other foot, trying to relieve the pain, when it happened –

Shadows moved rapidly around my room, dizzyingly fast. The security system did not make a sound. No one entered my apartment, and whatever phenomena I was experiencing did not trigger the alarm. Maybe I was in such pain that my mind was playing tricks on me. Was I seeing things? No. The shadows were real.

Strigoi. They finally manifested themselves, and they came, called by my pain. They didn't look like anything describable, other than black shadows of no particular shape. I was certain that even if I were in total darkness, they would still be the blackest things I would see.

"Hello," I said, not feeling afraid at all.

I felt as if they were trying to comfort me, telling me that they were at my service and not to worry about anything harming me. They didn't talk to me; I just understood the meaning of their intentions.

"Nice to meet you," I said, not sure if it made sense to them. "How do I summon you when I need you?"

I felt a feeling of togetherness, as if they'd always be there when I needed them. It was a good sense of assurance. From this point on, my squad of Strigoi guardians would protect me. I slept like a baby that night.

-VVV-

Special Agent Jane Kelly looked stoically at Agents Smith and Johnson. "I don't have good news. Homeland Security is closing the case."

"Why? We discovered incredible facts about Vlad Draculesti," said Smith.

"Yes, we did," agreed Kelly. "However, Vlad is not considered a terrorist, but a dangerous person for the FBI to investigate, along with François Le Beau and Angelique Brazeau, now that we know who she is. Thanks to Pratt."

"You mean that's it? We pack our bags and return to our home offices?" wondered Johnson.

"Yes. We need to wrap it up by the end of the week," said Kelly. "The NSA will continue the search for our three suspects and monitor Cat. Although the NYPD is investigating the limo murders, they'll find nothing. The FBI will continue looking for Vlad, Angelique, and François, and they're still searching for the real Veronica Seyler and Tiffani Arlin. And for Tom Brenner if he is alive, or his body."

"So that's it," said Smith. "There are four dead, if we include Vlad – or Brenner, if they killed him in Vlad's place – and we close the case?"

"We know that Cat is connected to François Le Beau and possibly Angelique Brazeau," said Johnson. "Cat also knows Veronica Seyler and Tiffani Arlin, and we do nothing about Cat?"

"Not us," said Kelly. "The NSA will keep an eye on Cat, and eventually she will lead us to some or all of them. That's it. Case closed."

-VVV-

François returned on the last day of June. I was so glad to see him, and I asked him to take me out to dinner. He was a perfect gentleman. We had lobster. I ate mine and his to give the impression that he had eaten. We drank two bottles of expensive wine, only half for me. I was giggling when I returned to the Fifth Avenue Apartment, via the Green Apartment. He went to his bedroom and promised to visit me for a nightcap.

353

Not finding me in the apartment's other chambers, he knocked at my bedroom door, and I opened it. I was wearing only a sexy, silky, burgundy babydoll. He stood there in his black shirt, only halfway buttoned, showing off his perfect pecs.

"*Chérie?*" He looked surprised.

"Baby, you can speak French to me all night long." I grabbed him by the belt buckle and pulled him into my bedroom.

The End

Thank you for reading my book. If you enjoyed it and would like to help other readers with your comments please write a review on Amazon. And of course I much appreciate your review as well. Amazon book link.

For more information about my books please visit sandru.com/blog/

Or visit me at my website: sandru.com and subscribe to my mailing list.

(Your e-mail will not be sold or used for spam)

Soon to be published:

The Pregnant Pope, by Mit Sandru, a Paranormal Thriller

Other books:

Vampire (Vlad V Series), by Mit Sandru, a Vampire Romance.

Meeting a vampire isn't something that happens every night, even on the New York City subways. Even in her wildest dreams Cat never expected to meet a vampire or survive an encounter with one. Instead, she becomes his confidant. Why is she so lucky?

Folding Reality, by Mit Sandru, a Paranormal, Time Travel Adventure.

Experiencing a new reality is just a paper-fold away for Mike the insurance salesman. But those realities are not by his choice and he ends up being crucified, or gassed at Auschwitz, or marooned in space in a Russian capsule.

Arboregal, the Lorn Tree, by D.G. Sandru, a Teen Fantasy and Science Fiction adventure.

Four young Americans are magically transported to a world where monsters roam the land, magnificent trees support all life, and an evil spirit hunts one of them to fulfill a deadly prophecy.

Escape from Communism, by Dumitru Sandru, a True Story and Commentary.

Life under communism is cruel and inhumane. Communist countries have a "Berlin Wall" around them, and the whole country is a giant concentration camp. I risked my life to escape from hell and reach freedom.

T-Shirts and other stuff:

Sandru's Shop or Sandru's Products

Visit my e-Gallery at:

http://dumitru-sandru.artistwebsites.com/

http://www.artistrising.com/galleries/Sandru

About Dumitru "Mit" Sandru

Dumitru "D.G." "Mit" Sandru was born in the greater area of Transylvania in the last century. He is an artist, composer, and author. He paints in the classical, surreal, and modern styles, and most of the music Dumitru composes is of the New Age flavor. As an author, he prefers to write Science-Fiction, Paranormal, and Teen/Children Fantasy & Sci-Fi novels.

Dumitru resides in California with his wife. They have one daughter and two grandsons.

Visit him at sandru.com